LIFE IS INEVITABLE

Daniel Santos

CONTENTS

Chapter One

Brennan splashed water on his face to hide the redness under his eyes. Even though this was supposed to be his best day according to his plan, he still had doubts. After all, everything he did always seemed to crash and burn. Once he returned to the classroom, he heaved a big sigh and unzipped his jacket. *What a day. What a shitty day.* With everyone in a zombie-like state in front of their computers, no one paid any attention to him, but maybe that was for the best. His leg was shaking as he glanced at the clock. Fortunately, the pointless drama that plagued this place wouldn't matter to him anymore, not after today. He took note of everyone around him. He locked eyes with a girl sitting to his left. Erica? Lauren? It didn't matter.

No one gives a fuck about your boy problems and daddy issues. Next was the guy to the right, Jeremy. *Nobody believes you're funny. You're just an asshole.* It pissed Brennan off just to see them. No matter where he went, life seemed to be filled with people who strived to make it harder for everyone else. Brennan took another glance at the clock. "Still got some time," he muttered. After a moment, he reached into his bag and pulled out the folded pages he had scrawled on the previous night and reread them. He gave a nod of approval and then re-folded the pages and placed them on his desk, hoping the teacher would read them.

He got up and his chair scraped the floor as it moved. He quickly walked around the other desk and made a beeline straight for his teacher.

"Excuse me, but could I go to the bathroom?" he asked her, and she looked up at him. Those soft eyes always showed understanding and forgiveness. She smiled at him.

"What were you asking?"

"Well, I just wanted to know if I could use the bathroom." Brennan smiled back at her and imagined what a woman like her would do if she knew what he was up to. "Yes, of course you can." She rummaged through her desk to look for a pass, but Brennan stopped her.

"It's alright. I won't take long," he told her. She pursed her lips but let him go anyway, and once he was out of the classroom, Brennan felt relief. This was finally going to be over. He pulled out his headphones and played music into his ears. He put his hands in his pockets, and as he walked through the halls, he would turn his neck to peer into some of the classes.

There was nothing out of the ordinary. Just some students listening to their teachers. He continued to walk out of the building and found himself looking back over his shoulder. *Do I really want to do this?*

Here he was standing outside. This was the first step in his plan, but he hesitated. "No," he whispered to himself. "I'm going through with this."

And with that, he left the school and headed straight for the store downtown. Although he was eager, he still walked like a turtle down the street. He wanted to take his time. The air felt like a warm blanket smothering his face, and he knew he had made the right decision to do it outside. Surely the air would provide some amount of comfort, but that hardly mattered anymore.

Brennan walked down the sidewalk by himself. He looked around, hoping to catch sight of someone, but there wasn't anyone there. No one, except him.

Alone again. In the back of his mind, the thought of loneliness still lingered, and he couldn't get rid of it. He shuddered at the thought of being alone. But why wouldn't he be alone? All those other kids at school didn't pique his interest. "Assholes," he'd call them. Brennan stopped for a moment and looked down at his feet. He pictured an image of himself at the top of a tree looking down. *Pretty soon.*

He picked up the pace and jogged down to the store. The sliding door flew open, and he cautiously stepped in. Suddenly, the world didn't seem so real anymore. It was like he was spectating through a camera rather than his own eyes. He took his headphones off and dropped them on the floor. "I don't need them anymore," he muttered.

At first, the store shelves were maze-like, but he had spent plenty of time there pondering his thoughts. He knew his way around the store now. He walked down the aisle past all the strangers he would probably never see again, and at the end he took a right turn and headed for the "tool section." *Where is it? Goddammit, where is it?* Brennan tried his best to focus but he just couldn't find it. *Where?*

"Hi, you need something?" A store employee came around the corner offering her services.

"I'm just looking for... for rope," Brennan said. He tried to hide the anxiety on his face, but that was harder than he thought, and the woman looked suspicious of him.

"Follow me," she said.

Brennan stopped in his tracks first. *Do I really want to go through with this?*

The lady continued to walk until she found some rope hiding in the back of a shelf. She turned back to find Brennan standing a few paces away from her.

"It's right here," she said, catching his attention. Brennan perked up and rushed towards her. She reached for the rope and handed it to him. She was holding it in front of her, but Brennan didn't make a move. His hands were shaking.

"Th-thank you," he stuttered. He snatched the rope out of her hands and began speed walking in the opposite direction towards the cash register. *I have to be fast!* he said to himself, but the woman ran directly towards him. She stopped him by placing a hand on his shoulder.

"Is everything alright?" she asked.Before answering, Brennan looked around him. Apparently, he had caught the attention of everyone in the store. For the first time in his life, all eyes were on him. He pushed her hand away and walked towards the register. She followed him, but he dismissed her.

"I'm just in a bit of a rush," he lied. Brennan dropped the rope on the counter and pulled out his wallet.

"Five dollars," the cashier said. Brennan pulled out a ten-dollar bill and handed it over. He hastily picked up the rope and began to walk out.

"You want the change?" The cashier called out to him, but he didn't answer.

It's time. Oh, it's time. Brennan repeated to himself. He wasn't walking like a turtle anymore.

As he walked, he fidgeted with the rope. He tried to tie all sorts of knots, but he couldn't find the right one to use.

Just like a snake, he said. *Imagine the rope is like a snake. It goes up and then down and...* He tried to remember the steps he learned but couldn't remember how to tie it. *Fuck, this'll be harder than I thought!* Brennan continued to mess with the rope until he found himself at his favorite park. *This is where it ends,* he told himself. He looked around and not one person was in sight. Here he was alone.

He walked over to a swing set and casually rocked back and forth. The creaking sound of the chains stabbed through the silence, and he sat there contemplating his plans. *I need to do this. There's no more room for people like me.* He continued to swing as he finally figured out how to tie the knot he wanted. The *hangman's noose.* He lifted it up to his face so he could get a good look at his artwork.

Brennan tugged at the rope to make sure it was tight enough. He stood up and dragged his feet towards a tree at the far end of the park. He stepped at the base of the tree and looked up. "Damn!" he said. This tree was just another big obstacle in his life. He jumped up with his arm stretched out to reach for a branch, but he couldn't do it. He jumped again but he was still too short. "Nothing ever comes easy," he muttered.

Brennan walked away from the tree and got into a running position. He stared at the branch he wanted to reach for. He sprinted forwards and jumped as high as he could. This time, he managed to get a good hold on a branch. By then he was breathing heavy, but he didn't want to waste any more time. He tied one end of the rope to the branch and put his head through the noose. He sat at the top of the tree and looked down. "This... This is it," he whispered.

But he didn't jump just yet. He kept his face pointed towards the ground and closed his eyes. He felt the sun shining on his face and imagined for a brief moment, what would happen after this. Would his family miss him? What would his teacher do after she read the letter he left on his desk? He could feel the tears coming through, but he stopped them from forming. *Why am I crying?*

Over the course of years, his tears had slowly vanished. Before, he could shed out entire oceans, but nowadays those oceans had been dried up. Maybe they'd been dry for too long. Maybe now was the time to refill his tear ducts so that he could clear his vision, but even with a clearer vision, his world view was still distorted, and so he leaped from the branch. With no regrets holding him back, it only took a split second for him to accept his fate. It felt like ages before he hung, but once he did, he felt the painful tug of the rope against his neck. His throat made a disgusting sound as it tried to get air. Naturally he felt the need to struggle, but he tried his best not to. However, he gave in. His body began to shake violently, desperate to breathe again. Eventually, it slowed down, and he became real still. His body was swinging from side to side. There was a growling sound coming from the pit of his throat, and after some time, that noise faded away.

Then his heart stopped beating.

Olivia was staring out the window, hoping to find something interesting. She rested her cheek in her hand and heaved a sigh. She smiled and exhaled as best she could. She could feel herself slipping away, but she didn't bat an eye.

Just a little longer. She slouched in her seat and continued to watch her teacher, Mr. Jefferson, lecture. As always, he was so lively and energetic. The students, especially the girls, watched attentively, even Olivia. The way he expressed himself through his writing was enough to garner her admiration, and the calm yet stern voice he had reminded her of her father, but he stopped talking and looked at her.

"Olivia, why don't you tell us how a writer can build suspense for their story." She smiled at him and stood up. "How about instead of keeping things vague, we let the audience know what's happening and –?"

"But what did we say about 'Show, don't tell'?" he asked her.

The other girls let out a giggle and Olivia blushed. That had to have been the tenth time this semester that she spoke without thinking.

"Hold on –" Olivia was quick to argue.

"Oh, I got it," Jessica called out as she raised her hand.

"Yes?" Mr. Jefferson said, pointing to her.

"How about we keep things a little vague and let the tension build up and hit the reader with something unexpected like a twist." Jessica smiled at their teacher, but gave Olivia a nasty look.

"Thank you," he said, "that's good enough."

"Better luck next time!" the girl teased. Jessica always stole the spotlight away from her in the most embarrassing way.

Olivia blushed and she felt like hiding away in a closet. *No, not this time.*

"Olivia, you can sit down now."

"Now hold on a minute, Mr. Jefferson," she quickly stammered out.He raised a brow and looked back at her with a newfound interest. "Yes?"

"I've heard of a scenario where two characters are talking, and there's a bomb under the table. We could keep things vague and let the bomb go off to surprise the reader, or we could –"

"Just stop talking already," Jessica teased. "It's annoying!"

"Shut up, Jessica!" Olivia snapped.

"Mr. Jefferson," she pleaded, "she can't speak to me that way!"

But Mr. Jefferson just held his hand up to silence them. "Let's just hear what you have to say," he said, pointing at Olivia.

"Th-thank you," she said. "The scenario asked, what if we let the audience know there's a bomb under the table? That way they feel anxious about when it goes off. That way, they'd be praying that the characters figure out the severity of the issue. The audience would want the characters to know what they know."

"I suppose that could work," he stated. "But it would be better suited for films rather than novels." Olivia sat back down. All she'd wanted to do was leave an impression on him before she went away. To just have someone, anyone, appreciate her, but again, she'd failed.

Jessica and all the other girls were eyeing her now, and she felt exposed. Everyone else turned to look at Mr. Jefferson, except for Jessica.

"You dumb slut!" she whispered in Olivia's ear. But rather than saying anything, Olivia just scooted her chair away and relaxed a bit. She crossed her arms over her desk and put her head down. *I just have to wait a little longer!* she told herself. Olivia's breath began to shake. She made sure to suppress her feelings, but it felt like she was a magnet for catching everyone's eyes. Her body began to wiggle, and she felt scared. *Why me? Why me?* she quietly cried.

Jessica's ears perked up at sound of her sobbing. She reached down to the floor and grabbed her bag. Her fingers nimbly searched through it to find some paper, and once she did, she smiled. "Hey, Olivia!" she said, grinning.

However, Olivia kept her head down.

"Hey, hey!" she kept pestering, but Olivia didn't move as she pretended not to hear anything. "Hey, look over here!" Jessica started nudging her, but she didn't move.

"Please stop!" Olivia pleaded, but Jessica slapped her hand to demand her attention.

"That hurt!" Olivia said, but when she finally lifted her head, she saw Jessica holding a ball of paper. She aimed it right at her and hit her on the cheek.

"Of course," Olivia muttered. Once Jessica turned away, Olivia leaned back in her chair. She put a hand over her stomach and whimpered. *This hurts more than I expected!* She ran her hands up and down to her stomach to find the source of the pain.

Once Jessica caught wind of this, she turned to face her.

"What's the matter?" she teased.

Olivia gave a sigh and closed her eyes. "Just shut up, okay?" she begged.

"Whatever," Jessica said.

The class went on and Olivia's eyes began to feel heavy. She would let out tiny groans of pain as she tried to stay quiet.

It's not fast enough. Olivia reached down to try to find her bag, but she felt nothing except for air. She looked down and saw only the floor. *Where the hell did those pills go?* She scanned the room until she felt the sharp stinging sensation in her head. "Shit!" she hissed.

"And as I was saying, this author –" Mr. Jefferson stopped teaching and looked at her. "Is there something you'd like to add?" he asked.

Olivia turned her gaze towards him, and out of her peripheral vision she noticed her classmates glaring at her.

"Sorry, I didn't mean to be so loud," she said.

Mr. Jefferson eyed her as though he were suspicious. "Right..." his voice trailed off.

After that, he resumed teaching, and Olivia smacked her hand against her forehead and heavily breathed out. She used her trembling hands to wipe the sweat off her face.

Maybe if I take more, it'll go faster. Olivia quickly and quietly reached into her pocket and pulled out a zip locked bag. Inside it were two white pills. "Who knew overdosing would be this painful!" she muttered. She tore open the bag and the pills dropped to the floor, sounding like marbles. "Shit!" she said looking down. She slowly bent over to pick them up, but Mr. Jefferson caught her in the act.

"Stop right now!" he yelled at her.

She sat upright and looked at him.

"You know that any medication I find on a student must be reported," he said.

Olivia never broke her gaze, and her mouth didn't move.

"Well, do you have anything to say?" Mr. Jefferson questioned, but Olivia didn't respond. She watched him leave the front of the class and walk over to the phone on his desk. He picked it up, and his fingers began stabbing the keypad.

"Oh, I didn't know you were a druggie!" Jessica laughed. "Go on, pick up those pills. They're probably for birth control."

The entire class burst out laughing at her joke.

Olivia felt too sluggish to respond. Time seemed to be slowing down and she fell to the floor. Her body made a loud thudding sound as she rolled over on her back. At that moment Olivia's fall was the only sound anyone heard. Her ears didn't pick up on any noise, and her eyes began to shut. She felt swelling in her stomach, and it traveled up her throat, causing her to vomit everything out. Her body jerked up and down when the puke shot through, but eventually she stopped moving. Her eyes began to close, and her heart stopped.

Brennan awoke from a deep sleep. His head was propped up against a wall, and when he opened his eyes, he looked around. The floor was made up of tiles, and metal benches were spread out against the wall. Judging by the complete darkness, he knew he must be underground. He thought back to the subway stations he used in the city. There was a resemblance here, except this place seemed older and dirtier, like an old-fashioned train station. He coughed hard and felt his neck. His fingers ran across the dent left behind by the rope.

What the fuck? He stood up and dusted himself off. The lack of a light source made Brennan feel like a blind man. He reached into his pocket and pulled out his phone to use as a flashlight, and walked aimlessly in different directions. His heavy feet were banging against the tiled floor, but he didn't see anything. He turned left, then right, but there didn't seem to be anywhere to go. At random, he would choose a direction and follow it. His footsteps echoed from wall to wall, and the rats scurried alongside him. *Where the hell am I?* he asked himself. He remembered his old days back in Sunday school. *Shouldn't I be in Hell right now?*

Olivia's footsteps echoed through the station, and the pain in her head didn't do much to help. She held her arms out in front of herself to feel the walls, or anything else she might run into. Her fingers ran up and down the tiles. Her feet scraped themselves against the ground, but she still moved forward. She felt a pounding in her chest after her first baby steps, and after a while it became more apparent. She tried to find her way around the place, but it seemed to be impossible here in the dark. She ran her hands up and down her pockets, but all she felt were her legs.

"Where's my damn phone?" she muttered. Olivia began recounting the events that happened. "First the classroom and then —"

Her eyes popped out at the memory. She felt her stomach and throat, but everything about her body seemed normal. The taste of vomit was non-existent, and the abdominal pain was gone. She began to push down on her belly to make sure she didn't feel anything, and she really didn't. *This is really messed up!* she told herself. She leaned against the wall and slid to the ground. She started shaking again as she began to breathe rapidly. *Breathe in and out,* she slowly told herself. *This is unreal. This is so unreal!* She laid a hand over her chest and tried to act normal again. *Oh God, where am I?* The brief thought of being lost heightened her senses and she started to hyperventilate. *No one's here!* She put her hands over her face and wept. Here she was, alone, and confused, just like the rest of her life.

Brennan came to a fork in the station. He shone his light at three corridors that presented themselves to him. All three were dark and misty, and not one looked different from another. He stood in front of them and thought about which hallway to choose.

There's no way to know for sure. Brennan pointed a finger in one direction and then slowly moved it in another. He would promise himself to take one path but then reconsider. "It's no use!" he muttered. He pulled his phone up to his face and entered his password. He looked at the top right corner of the glowing screen and saw the image of a tiny phone with an "x" over it. "No signal!" he said. Again, he looked down each corridor, but didn't make a move.

Suddenly, he jumped at the sound of a rat scurrying across the floor. He looked down and noticed dozens of tiny pebbles. He kneeled to pick one up and held it in between his thumb and index finger. He stared down the corridor right in front of him and wound up his arm. He hurled the rock down in a straight line and heard it bounce off a wall.

That's a dead-end. He went down again to steal another pebble and threw it down the corridor to his right.

Olivia's ears picked up the sound of a rock making a landing in the distance. She stood up and walked blindly in the direction she believed it had come from. As she moved, she heard the sound of another rock flying towards her. This time it smashed against her left eye.

"Ouch, what the hell was that?" she cried. She heard footsteps coming in her direction, along with a bright beam of light. She put her arm out in front of her face to shield herself.

"Hey!" a voice called out. Olivia's heart started racing again and she felt uneasy. She took a few steps backwards.

"Come back here!"

Rather than obeying the command, she turned around and started running back the way she came from. She moved as fast as the rats, but her feet echoed much louder than she hoped.

Run, run! she told herself. Olivia made her way straight down the corridor but couldn't find anywhere to hide. *Oh fuck, what am I going to do?* She made the decision to stand her ground and wait for the strange man to make his way towards her.

Brennan continued to shine his flashlight down the hall and follow the obscure apparition he saw. He could've sworn that he heard feet clambering against the floor, but he couldn't get a good look at who those feet belonged to. Was he just chasing a ghost? He slowly tiptoed forward, trying to not to make a sound.

Where are you? Who are you?

Eventually, he heard heavy breathing as he got closer and soon, a feminine figure came into view. He saw a young girl that he guessed to be about his age. She was clutching her chest with one hand while using her other arm to shield her eyes. Brennan dimmed the gleam of the flashlight on his phone, and cautiously walked towards the girl. "Finally, another person." he said. "How'd you get here?"

However, instead of answering his question, she smacked his palm out of the way and took a few steps back. "Back off!" she yelled. Her voice was wavering, and Brennan caught a glimpse of tears running down her face. "Go away!"

"Hey, relax!" Brennan told her as he gradually inched forward. "I'm just as confused as you are."

"I don't know you!" she cried.

"I just think it'd be best to work together. Maybe we can tell each other how we got here, and figure things out from there." Brennan continued to make his way closer to her, inch by inch. Once he got close enough to touch her, she fell backwards on her bottom.

"I said, go away!" she screamed.

"Just listen to me! We can both get out of here!" Brennan reached his hand down to help her up, but she didn't take it. He took a knee to get his face level with hers. "Let's work together," he said gently. He held out his hand once again, and this time she placed hers in his. He helped her up and she dusted herself off. The girl sniffled and used her sleeve to wipe her eyes.

"My name's Olivia," she muttered.

Brennan eyed her and smiled. "Well then, I'm Brennan. Now, can you tell me how you got here?" He pulled his phone to his face and changed the settings on the flashlight. He fidgeted around with it until the light became as strong as it was before.

"I just woke up here." She turned her head to the floor as she said that, and Brennan figured she wasn't telling the complete truth.

He walked past Olivia and told her to follow him. Together they continued to explore the dark corridors of the train station.

"So, you said you just woke up here?"

Olivia thought back to her experience in the classroom, and nodded her head. "Yeah," she lied.

"Well, that makes two of us," Brennan muttered.

"What was that?"

"Nothing, I just woke up here too."

Olivia heard his voice trail off and she looked up at him, sensing the lie in his voice. She made sure to take in every bit of him she saw. For all she knew, he seemed like a normal guy. There wasn't anything special about him. Just black hair and brown eyes, like the rest of the human population, but there was one thing that intrigued her. She stared at the mark that went around his neck. She lifted her hand to feel it, but Brennan grabbed her wrist mid-air.

"What are you doing?" he asked.

Olivia blushed and withdrew her hand. Of course, she had done something without thinking, again.

"I – I don't know," she sighed. "It's just that I see a mark on your neck. It's purple. Was it a bruise?"

Brennan kept his mouth shut and gave her a pat on the head. "Don't worry about it," he told her. He moved his eyes up and down her body from head to toe. *Red head and brown eyes.* To Brennan, her hair was the only thing that made her unique. Otherwise, she looked just like any other girl.

Olivia caught him staring at her, and she gave him a nasty look.

"You seem mad," Brennan commented.

"Well, you don't have to stare!" she retorted.

"But you can stare at me?" They both stopped dead in their tracks and glared at each other. Olivia pouted her lips, but Brennan forced an awkward smile.

"Forget about that," Brennan muttered. "Come on – let's keep going. This hall can't go on forever."

He continued to take the lead and she followed him without any objection, and so they traveled together for the next few minutes.

"Wait!" Brennan held out his arm to stop Olivia from moving forward. "Do you hear that?" he asked her.

Both of them stopped and stayed silent. They heard the noise of hundreds of voices talking.

"It's pretty close," Brennan said. "It's probably just a few feet in front of us."

"Should we go?" Olivia asked.

"I don't see why we shouldn't. If there's other people, then we could at least ask some questions. Maybe they can tell us how we got here."

"Or maybe not. I mean, we just woke up here without a clue. You think they'd help us? What if we're here because of them?"

"Well, do you have any other ideas?"

"How about we just ignore them and go through the other corridors."

"I came to a fork in the hall earlier. I can guarantee you, they don't lead anywhere."

"But we can't just –"

Without letting her finish, he already made up his mind. He took her hand, and together they ran in a straight line down the hall.

The sudden act of her hand being squeezed made her feel uncomfortable. Olivia never liked having other people touch her, and the speed at which he moved made her struggle to keep up.

At the end of the hall, they saw a door with a small window, through which came the warm glow of a candle on the other side.

"Just this way!" Brennan said excitedly. He barged through the door and realized they weren't alone. There were dozens of people walking about.

"Where are we?" She sounded awed.

Brennan looked around and saw a ticket booth as well as multiple trains speeding through the station.

"That's our way out of here!" he said, pointing to the tracks.

Olivia took a glance at the trains and her eyes lit up.

Brennan examined the ticket booths and felt his pockets for his wallet. "Shit," he muttered.

Olivia turned to face him. "What?"

"I don't have my wallet," Brennan said. "How are we supposed to buy our tickets?"

"Brennan, look!" Olivia pointed out two signs above each booth. One was clearly labeled "Heaven" while the other was labeled "Hell".

"What's that supposed to mean?" Brennan muttered.

Neither one of them could come up with an answer.

A short, white-haired young man in a suit made his way towards them. He looked up at the two and gave a big smile. "Hi!" he said.

"Oh, hello?" Brennan said as more of a question.

"Welcome to Purgatory!" the young man blurted out.

"What do you mean?" Olivia asked.

"You're both here awaiting to be sent to your next destination, correct?"

"Listen here," Brennan laughed, "we just want our tickets and then we'll leave."

The young man grinned and pulled out two shiny tickets from his pockets. "Congratulations!" he happily exclaimed. "God has decided to give you two a second chance."

"I don't know what you're talking about," Brennan said.

The young man's jaw dropped, and he stared at them without breaking eye contact. "So, you haven't realized?" he muttered.

"Realized what?" Olivia asked.

"You're both dead, but don't worry – you've been given a second chance." He kept his upbeat personality even as he said that and showed his teeth with a big smile.

"Alright, just give us the damn tickets!" Brennan demanded. He reached to snatch them, but the young man put them behind his back.

"Not so fast!" he told them.

"Look, we don't know what you're talking about, but we want to get out of here!" Brennan tried to reach his arm around him, but the man bit his fingers.

"Ouch, what the fuck!"

"Both of you must listen to me now. You two were brought here because you're dead," the man said in a more serious tone.

"Bullshit!" Brennan retorted.

"Now, I know that sounds insane but trust me on this. You've both committed suicide."

Brennan and Olivia took a moment to pause and think.

Once their faces turned serious, the young man smiled at them once again.

"Believe me now?" he asked.

Neither Brennan nor Olivia spoke a word.

"Now I need you two to listen to me very carefully," he said. "I'm your angel, Haniel, and these tickets will take you back to your bodies. Isn't that great?" Haniel presented both tickets in front of them, and Brennan eagerly snatched one up and walked towards a train.

"Hold on a minute!" Haniel said.

Despite the sudden good news, Brennan stopped with his face in a small, tight smile. Of course, he went through all the trouble in the world to kill himself, just for his efforts to be in vain.

Despite asking for him to stop, Haniel didn't say anything. Instead, he just smiled and Brennan assumed he was waiting for a response.

"That's very generous of you," Brennan said, "considering that you don't seem to be the type of person who holds that kind of power."

"Well actually, I'm just a messenger! It's God who decided to give you a second chance! Once you're brought back to life, you'll be able to do all those cool things like eating, sleeping, going to parks, meeting friends and..."

The longer Brennan had to listen to him, the more it felt like his ears were bleeding. The strong urge to retreat into isolation consumed him, and Olivia wasn't at all impressed. She held a strong gaze to the ground, her heart beating heavily. "And then we could meet up and –"

"Alright, I get it," Brennan interrupted Haniel. "Jesus, you talk too much."

Brennan noticed Haniel's face droop when he used Jesus's name in vain. After that, he immediately got in a line to get on a train.

Olivia ran after him, clutching the other ticket in her hands.

"Is this goodbye?" she asked Brennan.

"Doesn't matter," he said. "Besides, you didn't seem too eager to meet me earlier."

Olivia frowned and looked defeated. She looked up to him with puppy dog eyes. "I had this idea that we should keep in contact, so we can talk to each other when we wake up. After that we can figure out what to do next, but then again..."

Brennan looked at her, but he still wasn't able to make eye contact. Her eyes were simply too low. "I thought it would be a good idea, but I might be wrong."

Olivia shook her head as though it would rinse away her doubts.

Brennan folded his arms across his chest and let out a sigh. Right now, all he wanted to do was to be alone as quickly as possible, so he reluctantly gave Olivia his phone number.

"Call me when you wake up," he told her. After that, Brennan left her and boarded a large train that had just pulled up. Once he got inside, he found himself in one room. It seemed like a private jet with an interior of nice, polished wood and comfy red seats.

Brennan sat down and waited for the train to move. He heard the loud whistle sound and then it began to speed along the tracks. He looked back through the window and saw Olivia staring at him; he raised his hand to wave goodbye as he left the station.

*

Brennan laid back in his seat and pulled out the ticket from his pocket. He looked at the name. It read "Olivia Benning".

"Wh-what?" he stammered. He stood up and turned his head towards the driver. "Hey, I have the wrong ticket!" he yelled.

The driver turned around. Sure enough, it was Haniel.

"You should've checked it before snatching it out of my hand!" he laughed aloud.

"This isn't funny! Turn this train around!" Brennan demanded.

Haniel faced him and winked before the train jerked forward and picked up its pace. "Just hold on for the rest of the ride!" Haniel chuckled.

*

Olivia was jostled out of line by one of the many bystanders waiting to be ferried away. They made no hesitation to get in line, and they fought off anyone who stood in their way. She tried to keep her distance and avoid any sort of conflict. She scanned the area and saw a bench off to the side of the line. As the people in front of her continued to push and shove, she broke off from the rest of them. Olivia headed towards the bench and laid back on the wood. She closed her eyes, letting herself feel the air blowing from the oncoming train. *What a day*, she told herself. She opened her eyes and waited until she saw the next train. While she sat there, her right leg shook in anticipation. *Just a little longer*, she told herself. Her eyes were staring intently at the train tracks until her ears picked up on the sound of a cane approaching from behind. She took a moment to turn her head and saw an elderly woman making her way towards her.

She smiled, showing a mouth devoid of teeth. "Do you mind if I take a seat?" she asked.

"Not at all," Olivia said. She scooted herself to one end of the bench and the elderly woman sat down.

She chuckled at herself and rested the cane on her lap. "Even in death, I still need this thing," she laughed.

"What do you mean?" Olivia asked.

The woman grinned, showing off her gums. "Died at the ripe old age of 109," she chuckled and put a hand on Olivia's shoulder. "Why are you here? You're so young."

Olivia looked down in shame. Deep down, she knew she had made the biggest mistake in her life. She covered her eyes with her hand and cried. At first it was soft, but the sound of her sniffling started to become obvious.

The lady ran her hand around her shoulder as she tried to comfort her. "Don't worry," she said. "I've heard that Heaven is a lot better than this place." The woman pulled out her train ticket and showed it to Olivia. She scooped it up and stared at the words. *"Heaven"* it read.

Olivia showed a weak smile and handed it back to the woman.

"Where are you going?" the lady asked.

"I'm going home," Olivia said. She handed her ticket over, and the elderly woman read it.

A tiny train came into view and stopped in front of the bench. The door slid open and Haniel was waiting.

"Come on in!" he said. The woman returned the ticket and Olivia boarded the train. The woman waved her goodbye.

"I hope you continue to live your life, Brennan."

Olivia furrowed her brows as the sliding door closed. What was she talking about? Olivia sat down on the red sofa attached to the wall of the train. She laid down and held her ticket out in front of her. *"Brennan Claufield"* it read. Her eyes grew wide as she realized what was about to happen.

She sat straight up and looked out the window. She walked towards it and leaned her head on the glass.

This isn't over, is it?

Chapter Two

Olivia's eyes popped open. She was on a gurney in a white room. She lifted her head to look around. The heart rate monitor was attached to an electrocardiogram, and nothing about it seemed to be out of the ordinary. Her heart was beating at an average rate and only increased when she realized what had just happened.

I died, she told herself. She used her elbows to push her torso up, but coughed when she felt the burning agony of an injury to her neck. She ran her fingers around her throat and felt an indentation had left itself there. She lay down and stared at the ceiling. "Am I still me?" she muttered. She began patting down the sides of the gurney until she felt a small remote dangling from a cord. She brought it to her face and saw a shiny red button. She squeezed it, summoning a nurse.

While she waited, Olivia sat up and threw her legs over the side of the bed. She reached her hand under her hospital gown to tear the wires off, but she felt something odd. Her chest was made up of firm muscles that weren't there before. She used a finger to pull the shirt away from her chest and she peered down. It was flat and strong.

I'm Brennan. Eventually, Olivia finally got around to tearing off those wires and when they lost contact with her skin, the monitor turned red and began beeping wildly. She casually dropped the wires off to the other end of the bed and sat on the edge of the mattress. Her eyes drifted around the room, until they rested on the window. The entire parking lot was dark except for the streetlamps that shone down on the cars. When looking at the license plates, Olivia realized that every vehicle in sight was from Florida. The idea of being this far from home made her shudder. She thought about her mother, and how they were never the same since her father passed. *I need to see her again. Brennan and I need to switch bodies.* From there, she decided that she would get to Brennan as soon as possible to solve their issue. She waited patiently for the nurse to arrive.

After one more minute, Olivia heard someone grip the handle of the door. She focused in on the doorway as a nurse in a set of blue scrubs came walking through, along with a young woman trailing behind her.

"You're finally awake," the nurse said. The nurse gave a sheepish smile and walked over to a drawer at the other end of the room. Olivia stared at the young woman who was tagging along. She wore blue jeans and a black shirt with a gray hoodie to go over it. She left her jacket unzipped and had a book bag strapped across her chest. She smiled with tears in her eyes and ran to embrace Olivia. Olivia jumped at the unexpected display of affection, and she made no move to return the favor.

"I love you," the woman said. She pulled Olivia closer and ran her fingers through her hair. The woman pulled back and gazed into her eyes. She put her hand over hers and whispered, "We all love you, Brennan."

"Mom?" Olivia said as more of a question. The woman looked at her in bewilderment. *I'm an idiot.* This woman seemed too young to be his mother, maybe she was a girlfriend?

"Yes, I love you. Even Mom loves you," the woman said. She gave Olivia another gigantic hug and patted her back.

"Um... thanks," Olivia said.

The young woman let go of her embrace and turned away. "She can't be here right now, but you still have me," she said with her voice trailing off.

"Do you know what I did?"

"Yes, I know suicide is an intense feeling, but we can help you."

Even though Olivia had a clear memory of her death and the train station, the doubts that lingered in her mind were still very present. *This is real. Not a fever dream. We did kill ourselves.*

The woman averted her eyes with tears streaming down her face. Olivia stood up, but the nurse came around the bed with an instrument to check her blood pressure. She hastily put the strap around Olivia's arm and went through the whole process.

For the first time in a while, Olivia felt her blood pumping, and she felt alive again.

The nurse undid the strap and walked out of the room. "I'll give you some time with your sister," she said before shutting the door behind her.

Sister? Olivia had always been an only child. Her face turned into a mix of confusion and an ounce of eagerness. Brennan's sister could be the key to more knowledge about him and thus, help her understand his life better.

"Listen, let's try to work things out," Brennan's sister said. "I know you haven't been feeling that well, and I haven't been around, but... let's put the past behind us."

Olivia didn't try to continue the conversation. Instead, she got up and started pacing around. *What do I do? Am I stuck in this body forever?* She began to bite her nails and tremble.

The woman picked up on her odd behavior and started making shushing noises as she made her way towards her. "Everything's going to be alright," she whispered.

"I don't even know your name," Olivia muttered to herself.

"Who are you talking about?"

Olivia stopped and stared, not knowing what to say. "I – uh..." she stuttered. "What's your name?" Olivia felt genuine fear after asking her question. Who wouldn't know their sister's name?

Unsurprisingly, the woman had no idea how to respond to that. "What are you talking about?" she asked.

Both of them paused and the room was filled with silence.

Olivia could feel herself starting to hyperventilate and sweat began to form around her neck. Her eyes watered and she fell over into the woman's arms.

"I want to go home," Olivia stated. "I want this to be over. I want to be myself again!" Olivia was referring to her real body, but the woman didn't know any better. For all she knew, she was talking to Brennan and simply listening to his ramblings. Olivia tightly gripped her shirt, and wiped her eyes on it. "Take me home," Olivia quietly cried.

The woman cuddled her like a baby and wiped her tears. "I know things have been hard on you, but –"

"Just take me home!" Olivia screamed.

The woman sighed as she knew she was about to disappoint. "We can't do that just yet. You'll have to stay in the psych ward for a while and get some counseling."

Olivia cried harder and the woman made sure to hold her as tightly as possible. She slowly and steadily walked Olivia back to the gurney and helped her rest her head for a while. She pulled the white sheets over her body, covering Olivia from her neck all the way down to her toes.

Olivia rolled over on her side and pushed her hands under the pillow. She curled up and tried to cover her body, looking for a sense of security.

The woman sat at the end of the bed, right next to Olivia's feet. She pulled out a small phone from her pocket and dialed a number. The phone buzzed as she held it to her ear, expecting to be directed towards a voicemail, but on the other end, a feminine voice started speaking.

"Mom, it's me, Nora. Brennan and I are in the hospital right now. Could you –?"

Nora was quickly interrupted by the woman. Olivia's ears could faintly pick up on the lady's voice, but to her it just sounded like incoherent whispering. Nora hung up the phone and put it back in her bag.

Olivia felt a small amount of hope just then. *That phone... Could she use that to call Brennan?*

Nora placed a hand on her leg. "You don't need to worry about anything else right now," she whispered. She leaned over and gave Olivia a kiss on the cheek. After that she got up and headed towards the door. She looked back and smiled. "I'll come again tomorrow." Nora pulled the door open and stepped out, leaving Olivia alone with her thoughts.

Olivia curled her body up into the fetal position and hugged her pillow. She gripped it in front of her face, almost to the point where she could smother herself. She cried an ocean of tears into the soft fabric. This was a new sort of pain she had yet to feel. Although she resented her past life, this was not something she wanted. To be thrown into a new cycle of torment in a brand-new world wasn't exactly her idea of peace.

Olivia's thoughts were racing around furiously in her head. What did her real family think of all this? Surely everyone in town would know of the high school girl that had overdosed, and oh God... If Olivia took Brennan's ticket, there was no other conclusion. He must be in her own body right now. What could he be doing? Olivia tried her best to shut out the thoughts that were intruding, but that just wasn't who she was. Her mind wasn't like static on a television. There was always something going on in there. She closed her eyes and whispered a quiet prayer. Was there supposed to be a special word or phrase to say? Maybe "Amen"? Olivia put her hands together with her fingers pointed up. "Amen," she whispered. She went back to hugging her pillow and fell asleep, with her cheek resting against the cushion.

Olivia woke up the next day half expecting everything to be back to normal, but reality hit her like a truck when she realized she was in the same room. She lay in bed, feeling hopeless and afraid. What would she do now? It had only been a couple of minutes since she'd woken up and already, she was thinking of what to do next. Her body and mind were eager to leave, to start searching for Brennan, but when she realized that a plan was needed, she felt despair. Being stuck in a state and life she didn't know wasn't exactly the type of thing to put her at ease. Would learning about Brennan's life help or would running away be her best option? She closed her eyes and thought, but a game plan wouldn't surface.

Then the nurse came in, acting more optimistic than usual. "I think you should eat in the cafeteria today," she said cheerily.

Olivia reluctantly threw her legs over the side of the bed and stood up. She gradually made her way towards the nurse and followed her through a white corridor down to a set of double doors. Past the tiny windows on the door, Olivia could see another bland room with the same color scheme.

The nurse handed Olivia the tray and she went to hold the door for her. Once it swung open, she saw a room full of patients eating normally at their tables. Some were huddled together in small groups, but most of them were trying their best to create as much space as possible between one another.

The nurse directed Olivia towards a table at the center of the cafeteria, and once she sat down, the nurse invited herself to take a seat across from her. She searched her scrub pockets and pulled out two plastic pieces of cutlery. She handed them over to Olivia, but she didn't take them. Her mind was still pondering the situation she had gotten herself into. Surely, this wasn't something she could just undo. The nurse set the cutlery down in front of

Olivia. However, all she did was stare at the mush on her plate without breaking her gaze.

"Don't worry, things will get better," the nurse said, trying to comfort her.

"You don't know what I'm going through," Olivia responded.

The nurse pursed her lips and held Olivia's hands. "There are many people here just like you," she said.

"No, there aren't. Trust me, there aren't."

"I can guarantee you there are."

The nurse just wouldn't understand. Olivia felt like it physically hurt her ears just to hear her say that. She knew that there was no way anyone could comprehend her situation. She reached her hand out in front of her to grab the plastic spoon which she promptly used to scoop up the food and shove it into her mouth.

"How long will I be staying here?" Olivia asked with her mouth full.

"That completely depends on you," the nurse said. "The psychologist will have to evaluate you first and you'd have to show us that you're getting better."

Olivia rolled her eyes to make her distaste as clear as possible. "Just give me an estimate."

The nurse's eyes turned towards the ceiling as she thought about it. "Most people stay here anywhere from four to ten days."

Olivia spat out the food in her mouth and onto the plate. "Are you serious!" she yelled.

All the eyes in the room turned to face her as they heard her shriek.

"I can't wait that long! I need to see someone."

The nurse put a hand up to motion for Olivia to stop and stay silent. "Like I said, it completely depends on you. Every patient here is different."

Olivia left her food unfinished, and she picked up the plate to throw in the trash. She wiped her mouth with her arm and headed towards her room.

The nurse walked side by side with her. "The social worker will be here soon. You can talk to her about what happened."

"How soon?" Olivia asked. She kept her head low and her voice monotone, like a rain cloud was stalking her from the ceiling.

"Just be patient. She'll be here." The nurse patted Olivia on the back and ushered her into the room.

She made straight towards the bed and lay down.

The nurse proceeded to shut the door before she left, and it closed without a sound.

Considering that Olivia took enough pills to put herself into a coma, waking up immediately wouldn't be an option. Instead, Brennan was stuck in the train with Haniel. As the wheels rumbled against the tracks, tension filled the air. Brennan still had his pouty face, and Haniel did nothing but smile.

"I suppose I'll be waking up as Olivia," Brennan said, breaking the silence. He lifted the ticket to his face so that the name was facing him. As his eyes narrowed in, he noticed Haniel nod in the background. Brennan reread Olivia's name on the ticket multiple times as if that would change anything, but of course, it didn't. "Hey, Haniel."

"What?"

"Can you tell me more about this place?" There was a hard edge to his voice.

"You don't sound like you really care about that," Haniel said.

"I know. I just need to pass the time, and considering that this is your fault, you should help by keeping me entertained."

"What do you mean it's my fault?"

"You should've warned me that I took the wrong ticket. Now look where it led us."

"Well, at least you're on this cool train!" said Haniel in a cheery tone.

Brennan just sighed and sat back down on the red couch. When he closed his eyes to think of a future plan, he realized that he'd never asked Olivia where she lived, and considering that they were the only ones that knew about their situation, he couldn't think of anything else but meeting up with her. "So, can you start telling me about this place?" he asked Haniel.

"Oh, sorry, I forgot to talk about that. You just seemed so upset."

"I still am, but I just need a distraction."

Haniel sucked in an enormous puff of air before speaking. "Well, this place doesn't really have a name. Me and my angel friends just call it 'the in-between.' We get new patrons every minute of every day, but most of them end up going to Heaven or Hell."

"Why are Olivia and I different? Why do we have to go back?"

"When most people come here, they have some sort of peace or closure after dying. Despite what their next destination is, they've reached acceptance. You and Olivia are two of the few that haven't reached closure."

"Two of the few?" Brennan asked. "There are *more* people who've been brought back from the dead?"

"Yes, absolutely." Brennan noticed that rather than continuing with his cheery attitude, he was staring off into the distance.

"Hey, Haniel. This sounds like God put me on some sort of mission."

Haniel suddenly stopped staring and responded. "In a way it is a mission. You're supposed to find peace – whatever that may seem like – but for the most part, you have a lot of freedom."

"Then does that mean I can meet Olivia? Once I wake up, can I get to her?"

"I think so."

"In that case, I guess I'll just fix everyone's mess like I always do," Brennan pouted. "Since you're an angel working by God's side, I suppose you can tell me where Olivia has been living?"

"I can't exactly spectate everyone. I'm not God. I'm just an angel."

Brennan sighed and folded his arms across his chest. "You're fucking useless. You know that?" He bowed his head and tried to retrace the events that had just happened. He was hoping that Olivia had told him where she lived, or at least gave him a clue, but when he replayed their conversations in his head, nothing came of it.

Suddenly, he remembered the shirt she wore. It was a vague memory, but he did see a ginormous building protruding into the sky. The tip of it was pointed and the base seemed somewhat thin. *The space needle! She was wearing a shirt of Seattle's space needle. Maybe she lived in Washington?* He had nothing else to go on, so he decided that Washington was his best guess.

*

Olivia's body was resting in bed, but her mind was a whole different story. There were still so many questions left unanswered. She was completely oblivious when it came to Brennan's life, and she wondered if his family would suspect anything. What would they say when she didn't know their names, or didn't even recognize their faces? Olivia instinctually wanted to cry from the overwhelming amount of stress, but this time she kept her composure. *No more crying,* she told herself.

She began to wonder what was happening to Brennan. Did he adjust to her life already? Hopefully he didn't mess it up any more than it already was. Olivia wanted to know what her friends and classmates thought of her, but fear would find itself creeping into her mind. Maybe they wanted her dead, or they just didn't care whether she was there or not...

But what about Brennan's acquaintances? Just the idea of meeting new people horrified her, but Olivia felt a strong sense of curiosity when it came to Brennan. Would she be intruding, simply by living his life? Living his life would be like reading a personal diary, and she knew firsthand how embarrassing that was. After all, Jessica would be teasing her about everything she wrote. It was like having someone opening your head and reading your innermost thoughts.

Washington. He couldn't know for sure if she lived in Seattle, but at the very least there was a good chance she lived in Washington. Brennan had never left Florida before, so traveling across the entire country just to meet one girl seemed to be a ridiculous idea.

By now it had been a few hours since the train had departed, and Haniel was laying on the sofa across from him. He snored like a cartoon character with his mouth wide open. His white hair fell to the side and covered his face. Again, bitterness started to swell up within Brennan. *Lucky bastard. All he has to do is watch while I deal with this shit.* Brennan went back to his usual pose, with his head hanging low and his arms folded across his chest. His leg shook while his foot tapped the ground.

"Is something on your mind?" Haniel asked, after Brennan's tapping woke him.

"I'm always in need of something."

Haniel cocked his head to the side. "What does that mean?"

"Just forget about it. No one would understand anyway."

"You ever thought of opening up a bit more?"

Brennan turned his head away to avoid eye contact. He preferred to be alone. And when he managed to catch a glimpse of the world outside, he saw only darkness, but that darkness gave him a bad feeling. "Where the hell are we?" he asked.

"Remember when I said you haven't achieved closure in your life?"

"Yeah, but what does that have to do with this?"

"Well, a lot of our 'lost souls' end up here. They tend to wander around, searching for something that doesn't exist. I don't want to put any pressure on you, but if you don't achieve closure, you might end up here."

Brennan's eyes popped out for a moment. If his mission was to learn a lesson, then he'd truly been screwed over. Both the world of the living and the world of the dead seemed to be against him. "So, you're saying that if I don't do whatever it is I'm supposed to do, I'll end up like one of those sorry fucks out there?"

Haniel nodded his head.

Great. At that point, Brennan didn't know if being dead would've been a blessing. The longer the train lingered in that area, the more uncomfortable it made him. Brennan would occasionally fidget in his chair, and when Haniel offered words of comfort, he would immediately brush it off.

It wasn't until they noticed a bright light that everything seemed to calm down.

"Am I about to wake up?" Brennan asked.

Haniel shrugged his shoulders and the train went into the light.

For a while, Olivia laid in bed without saying a word, until she felt a tiny breeze of air coming through the opening of the door. Without turning her attention over to it, she just assumed that she knew who it was.

"You must be the social worker," Olivia said.

"Nope!" Came a friendly and cheerful voice.

This time Olivia lifted her head to get a good view of who it was, and she found Nora standing there, wearing the same clothes since her last visit.

"Nora," Olivia muttered.

"I told you I'd be back."

Olivia found a good hold on the remote by her bed and used it to make the mattress elevate itself. The bed creaked as it shifted, and Nora finally broke the silence when she briskly walked up to Olivia and playfully punched her arm.

Olivia gently rubbed the spot as though it hurt and she casually threw one of her own. "Hey, is there –?"

Before Olivia could finish her question, Nora told her to hold that thought as she reached into her bag. She pulled out a large roll of paper and then straightened it out, revealing it to be a poster. "Look at this!" she happily exclaimed. Right there printed on the page was a giant drawing of a teddy bear with a talk bubble that said, "Get well soon." All around the drawing were the names of people who signed it – none of whom Olivia knew at all. "See how much everyone loves you!"

Olivia tried to smile, but she held back. After all, this wasn't her life.

After some digging through her bag, Nora just so happened to be carrying tape with her. She tore off a few pieces and used it to stick the poster on the wall.

"There we go," she said, admiring her handiwork. "Hey, Brennan, I think you have another visitor." Nora grinned and gently punched Olivia's arm again like a child at school.

"Is it another social worker?" Olivia asked.

Nora turned her head in the other direction as a smirk started to etch itself on her face. "No," she said, looking down. "It's Mrs. Walker."

"Who?"

"You don't remember? You always told me how much you enjoyed her class."

Olivia realized how lost she was. This woman might've been close to Brennan, but Olivia never even knew she existed. "My teacher...?" Olivia said, confused.

"Well, yes, of course." Nora's eyes gave the impression that she was a bit bemused at Olivia's lack of interest.

"Wait, what class is this?" Olivia mistakenly used this chance to ask more questions, and the more she asked, the deeper she dug herself into trouble.

"Are you okay?" Nora asked. She put a hand over Olivia's forehead. "You're not that warm. Did they give you something? Medical marijuana?"

Olivia tried to suppress a laugh, but it came out as more of a grunt instead. "Maybe," she said, raising the pitch of her voice. "Just a little weirded out by everything." Her face lit up, and for the first time in a while, she gave a genuine smile.

It seemed like it was done out of pure instinct, but Nora took the time to give Olivia another big hug.

This time Olivia wrapped her arms around her and pulled her closer. Just like a baby in her mother's arms, she didn't want to let go anytime soon. Olivia took in her flowery scent and the presence of security Nora seemed to radiate. *I could get used to this.* Her legs felt like jelly, and she became weak and vulnerable. *Why would Brennan have ever wanted to leave his life behind? This amount of love was something that should be treasured.* "I love you," Olivia finally found the courage to say, and Nora squeezed their bodies even tighter together.

After going into the bright light, Brennan had some sort of out-of-body experience. He couldn't move, but he felt like his mind was awake. He lay in a hospital bed with an oxygen mask tightly secured to his face. From time to time, his eyes moved beneath his eyelids. They rolled around without stopping, and not another part of his body moved.

At one point a distraught man came in to visit. He clasped Brennan's hand and stared at him wavering. "Olivia, what did you do?" he said sadly.

Brennan gave a soft groan, but his body was still and lifeless.

"Olivia," the man whispered.

Although he didn't make a single move, Brennan could sense his presence. He tried to twitch a finger, but the action felt like lifting a truck. In the back of his mind, Brennan was still alive and functioning, but his body told him otherwise. The firm touch of a hand grazed Brennan's forehead, and it went away almost instantly.

After that ordeal, Brennan found himself to be standing in an endless white void. There didn't seem to be any walls. The area was vast, with nothing further off into the distance. At first Brennan only viewed what was in front of him, but when he turned his back, it was a whole different story.

Behind him he saw two children playing on a seesaw. They were hopping up and down without a care in the world. One child had white hair and was especially cheerful. She screamed with joy as the playground equipment flew her up into the air. On her way up she threw a hand reaching for the sky and she leaned back with a big grin on her face. On the other end of the seesaw was a boy with hair as dark as midnight. He still seemed eager to play, but his face wasn't as animated. He kept a calm demeanor and tried his best to keep the seesaw balanced. The two kids kept going at it, and Brennan felt strangely inclined to watch. He felt like a child looking into a candy store.

"Well, would you look at that," Haniel said, sneaking up from behind.

"Hey, Haniel –"

"Hey, yourself."

"Where the hell am I?"

Haniel chuckled and picked at the ground with his toes. "Let's just say you're almost awake," he laughed.

Brennan furrowed his brow and wondered what he had meant. *Almost awake?* "We went through some sort of weird adventure when using the train. After all that, shouldn't I at least be awake, or somewhere other than here? I mean, I did see a bright light. Isn't that supposed to mean something?"

Haniel gave a big, toothy smile and patted Brennan on the shoulder. "Don't worry. You'll wake very soon. Just enjoy your time here."

Brennan scoffed at him and then turned his attention back to the children. "Who are they?" he asked.

Haniel gave him a small nudge in the side and giggled. "Why don't you ask them." Without warning, Haniel skipped his way behind Brennan and gave him a great big push forward.

Brennan tripped and fell to the ground. There was a loud thud as he made contact with the floor, catching the children's attention. They boy stopped jumping and his weight kept his side of the seesaw down while the little girl was suspended in the air. The kids looked at Brennan and then back at each other. The girl gave the boy a short nod and then she leaped off the seesaw and scurried along towards him. The boy hastily followed behind her. Brennan slowly lifted his head up and was greeted by the image of the two wide-eyed children. The girl took Brennan's hand and helped him get up on his knees.

"Thanks," he said.

The children didn't say a word or make even the slightest noise.

"Uh..." Brennan felt the introduction of an awkward silence making its way in. "Who are you two?" he finally asked.

The little girl pointed a finger at her chest and said, "Life."

"You're who?"

"I'm Life," she said.

"Wait a minute," Brennan said, raising his hand. "Your name is 'Life'?"

The girl happily nodded, and she pointed a finger to the boy next to her.

"This is my brother, Death."

Brennan let out a laugh. He held his hand to his stomach since the laughter was sucking air out of him. His eyes began to tear up and he wiped away a drop with his thumb before regaining control. "I don't get it. I just don't get it," he said. "This whole day has just been a fucking shit-show."

The little girl cringed at the word "shit" and leaned over to slap him on the chest. "No!" she chided him.

"Alright, alright," Brennan said defensively.

Life took her brother's hand and led him towards the seesaw, ready to resume their playing. "Keep it balanced," she told him.

Death went to his end and sat down. The other side of the seesaw hung in the air and Life tried to hoist herself up, but her fingertips barely touched the seat.

"Wait there," Brennan called out to her. He stood up and gracefully walked towards her. He lifted her up from under her arms and raised her tiny body to the top of the seesaw. From there, Death hopped up and Life went down. Once her feet touched the ground, she didn't move, and neither did her brother.

"Hey, why did you two stop?" Brennan asked.

"We like it this way," Death told him.

Brennan gave him a weird look while a million thoughts ran through his head. *What a strange pair of kids.* "Why don't you two just play? You know, one jumps up while the other goes down?"

Death shook his head to say "no" and he averted his eyes towards his sister.

"If we did that it wouldn't be balanced," she said.

"Who cares?" Brennan argued. "Just let one person's weight take over the other. Simple as that."

"But if we do that it goes crazy," Life said.

Brennan thought for a minute. *What the hell is going on?* He wondered if these kids were actually kids, or just some ghosts playing tricks on him. Either way, his whole day had been nothing but a strange series of events that led him here. "What are you talking about?" he asked.

"If my brother doesn't stay still the ride goes up and down —"

"Isn't that what it's supposed to do?" Brennan interrupted.

"But then I could fall and he'd be lost."

"What do you mean, he'd be lost?"

"If I'm gone, he can't play. He needs me."

Brennan put a palm to his face and wondered what was going through the girl's head. "But you're not playing at all," he told her.

She gritted her teeth at his response and stuck out her tongue at him.

Brennan smirked at her response and stuck his tongue out at her too. He giggled a bit and then smiled at both of them. "I know you need each other, but if you never do anything, it gets boring. Nothing happens." Brennan eyeballed the kids to make sure they were still listening to him. Their eyes were glued to him. "This toy needs both of you to make it work," he lectured. "Don't be afraid. Just play like you did earlier."

Life hesitantly hopped up and Death hit the ground. After that he jumped up and it was Life's turn to go down.

"See? That's what I mean," Brennan said.

The children kept hopping up and down and Life quickly forgot about her worries. The enjoyment began to show itself on her face. Brennan could even see Death slowly letting a smile loose.

He lowered himself to the ground so he could take a seat as he watched the children play. "Isn't this better?" he asked them.

"It's really crazy!" Life called out to him.

"Well, when things seem insane, it might just be the way it's supposed to be. You gotta learn how to go with it and take control."

Life smiled and stared intensely at her brother as though she had a newfound confidence. She giggled, but her brother didn't do much to show his own enjoyment.

However, that's when Brennan turned his attention to him. "Come on, go enjoy yourself," he called out to him. "You're just as important as she is."

And as the kids kept playing, Brennan felt a small gust of air fly past him. Turns out Haniel was already making his way around. He stopped right next to Brennan and placed a hand on his shoulder. "You're like a whole different person now," Haniel told him.

"The kids just don't know how to play," Brennan muttered.

"You always seemed so tense."

"I try not to be... or at least I try not to be tense around kids."

"Oh, really?" Haniel gave him a strange a look as though he didn't believe him.

"I mean it," Brennan said. "Kids shouldn't have to deal with the bullshit life throws at them."

"Where's this coming from? You seemed pretty annoyed when we were on the train."

"Just forget about it."

"Well, now that you've brought it up, I just can't." Haniel smiled wide and exposed his canine teeth as though he were a vampire.

Feeling annoyed, Brennan took a moment to walk away.

By now, Life and Death were stuck playing an endless game with each other. The seesaw kept going up and down without anyone daring to make a stop.

Brennan laid back with his arms crossed behind his head to create a makeshift pillow.

"Enjoy your time here." Haniel's words echoed in Brennan's mind, and he knew that he should listen. This white space seemed more like a paradise than a prison, despite its emptiness. That emptiness was the exact thing that made this place so calm. Brennan found himself listening to Life's laughter and the creaking noise of the seesaw with a huge amount of amusement. He closed his eyes and relaxed, making sure to take in every bit of warmth and calmness radiating from his surroundings. What was this place anyway? There were no walls or bars to keep him here. Was it a room or just a void? But that didn't matter to him. Brennan just wanted to lie on his back and live in this moment forever. He slowly breathed in and then exhaled deeply through his nose, but something stuck out to him. He gradually heard faint whispers caressing his ears.

"Olivia, Olivia," they said.

An intense feeling of despair washed over him, and Brennan tried his best to shove it away.

"Olivia, Olivia." The voice was getting louder, making a grand entrance through his eardrums. Brennan made a whining noise similar to an infant, and his body began to kick frantically like he was drowning in a pool.

"She's waking up! She's waking up!" the voice yelled.

Brennan felt the feathery weight of blankets on his body and the laughter of the children began to fade away.

"No, no," Brennan's mind pleaded. "I want to stay. I want to stay here." He started to thrash his arms about, but he felt the sting of fluids pumping through his veins. His heart started pounding like it was ready to burst through his chest, and he made a loud gasp for air.

"She's almost here," the voice said.

Brennan's fingers began to twitch, and his muscles tightened as his body jerked upwards. A surge of electricity shot through him like lightning striking an antenna. After a brief moment of stillness, the same feeling came back just as soon as it had left. Eventually, Brennan heard the faint beeping noise of a machine, and that was when things began to die down. The voices were still talking, but they weren't as chaotic, and Brennan could feel their hands touching him. Some of them were firm while others were gentle.

It was at that moment that Brennan slowly opened his eyes. Standing above him was a team of doctors and nurses eagerly waiting for his arrival back to the world. He had just enough strength to turn his head and noticed one of the staff carrying a defibrillator.

"Good job, doctor," a nurse said off to his right.

The doctor gave Brennan a pat on the shoulder and went about his regular business to make sure Brennan stayed awake at this time.

A day had passed, and yet here she was. The atmosphere of the hospital hadn't changed much at all. Olivia still felt the chaos that was rampant throughout the psych ward, and the smell of disinfectant lingered under her nose. The thought of Brennan would sometimes pop into her head, and she'd feel a mixture of fear and confusion. How was she going to get back into her body? Could she even go back to her body?

He gave me his phone number.

Yes, his phone number. The only possible way she could have contacted him, but she was the one who had his phone.

"What if I called my number?" Olivia muttered. She began to formulate a plan, but she didn't have all the tools to execute it. That phone could be her savior, but where should she start looking? She sat at the edge of her bed, biting her nails. Time. She needed more time to figure things out. As always, Olivia thought up every little scenario that could happen. Maybe the nurses had her phone. Maybe she'd be able to call Brennan and work things out, or maybe there was no going back. Olivia closed her eyes and sighed.

What a mess. For a while, she did nothing but ponder her thoughts, but soon enough the door to her room gently creaked open and she turned her attention towards it.

A tall, beautiful woman with blue glasses came walking in. Her facial expression was flat, as though she were mad or annoyed, but the moment she smiled it seemed like everything changed. First impressions showed Olivia a grumpy woman, but that sweet voice and wide smile told her otherwise. She could look this woman in the eyes and see a childlike sense of wonder.

"It's good to see you again," she said.

"H-hi –" Olivia let out a short stutter. *Who? Who is she?* "I... I...." She tried to find the right words to say.

"I got the letter you left at your desk."

Olivia scratched the back of her head vigorously as she thought *What did Brennan do?*

"It's... it's very... I'd say... thoughtful..." The woman stammered out. She put her arm around Olivia and held her close. "You know, you can always come to me for anything. I'd never turn down a student, never."

"Thank you, Miss... Miss..." Olivia tried to think of a name. She raced through the events of Nora's last visit, and the name "Walker" resurfaced. "Ms. Walker," she said.

"Don't you worry about a thing anymore," Ms. Walker told her.

"Would you mind if I –?"

"If you what?"

"Would you mind if I take that letter back?" Olivia forced an awkward smile out. Maybe that letter would give her an insight into Brennan's life.

For a moment Ms. Walker paused, and her expression showed curiosity. Olivia realized that she must've been acting out of character for Brennan, but despite that, Ms. Walker just so happened to be carrying the note in her purse. She carefully pulled it out and handled it like it was a priceless treasure.

Before grabbing it, Olivia could see the small creases made in the paper and how worn out it was, as though it had been opened multiple times. "Thank you," she said as she took the letter and placed it under her pillow for later reference.

Out of nowhere, Ms. Walker's purse started to vibrate, and it made the bed wiggle.

"Oh, excuse me for a minute." She put her hand down her bag and pulled out a black cell phone that was eagerly buzzing for an answer.

A phone. That's exactly what Olivia needed. She stared intensely at the electronic device as she imagined all the things she could do with it. *I'll call Brennan. I'll call him.*

"Okay, I'll be on my way." Ms. Walker finished her call and put the phone back in her purse. "Sorry, but I have to go. We have a teachers' meeting. I'll come back later to visit." Just before she could walk out the door, Olivia called out to her.

"Wait," Olivia said.

Ms. Walker stopped and stood motionless.

"Can I use your phone, please?" Olivia asked. "I have to call a friend and tell them I'm fine."

Ms. Walker happily agreed and gave Olivia her phone.

She gratefully took it and held the device like it was gold. "Thank you so much," she said. She quickly flipped it open and dialed her number. She held it to her ear and listened to the phone ring. It buzzed and buzzed, but not once did she hear someone on the other end. It felt like her heart broke into pieces when she was directed towards her own voicemail.

"Hey, Bre–... I mean, hi, Olivia," she corrected herself. "I'm at the hospital right now. You should call me back later. You know your number." Olivia said this all while gritting her teeth. *He better answer me.* She ended her message, closed the phone and handed it over to Ms. Walker.

"I hope you feel better," Ms. Walker said.

"I hope so too," Olivia responded. After that, Ms. Walker left the room and Olivia was alone again. She took the time to lift up her pillow and take the note she had hidden underneath. She laid down and opened the letter. Her eyes ran across the beautiful penmanship and her fingers traced the dried cracks left behind on the page.

Dear Ms. Walker,

First off, I'd like to say that I'm truly grateful to have been a part of your class. Every day when I wake up, I just tell myself, I have to make it to my graphic design class. I just have to. Yes, it's at the end of the day, but that's not why I love it so much. You genuinely make it a great place for me, and I'm sure everyone else loves you too. I may feel like I'm burning in Hell, but your classroom is Heaven to me. I hate my school and peers, but I know for a fact that you have left an impression on me. I can tell that you care deeply about everyone that comes by, and I appreciate that.

As of right now I'm positive this will be my last day here. I don't know if anyone will miss me, but I'm sure that I'll miss you. Thank you for doing your best to make this a good year for me, but I've come to an important decision and it's one I have to make on my own. Just remember, it's not your fault. I made this decision. It's my burden to bear.

— Brennan

Olivia slowly and carefully folded the letter again and stuck it under her pillow. She put a hand over her mouth to suppress the sound of her cries as she tried to figure out what to make of it. Was it possible that she'd finally met someone she could relate to? She still couldn't believe it. She retrieved Brennan's letter and reread it to make sure she wasn't hallucinating. Her heart started racing, and it felt like it was going to burst out of her chest. Was there really someone out there that had the same thoughts as her?

"We're not that different," Olivia muttered. She wanted to cry out to him and talk to him, but the world had created a barrier between them. For the rest of the night, Olivia lay curled in a little ball, hugging her pillow until she fell asleep.

As always for the past few days, Brennan lay awake in bed, not knowing what to do. He rubbed his head hoping the pain would go away, but it never did. His body was drenched in sweat, even though his environment was freezing. For some reason it still felt like his body was a teapot being heated, and each time the doctor took his temperature, they'd see the thermometer spur up.

Goddammit, Olivia. What did you do to your body?

This whole situation was a new kind of hell, and Brennan was still wondering why he wasn't actually sent straight to Hell. Surely that would be more desirable than this. He reached over to the side of his bed to take the remote. He eagerly tapped the button that would elevate his head, followed by the one that would call for the nurse. And as the bed creaked to raise Brennan up like a mountain, the nurse came in to greet him.

"You called again?" she asked. "What's the problem?"

Brennan pushed himself up with his elbows and grinned. He opened his mouth but failed to conjure up any words, so he let out a halfhearted laugh.

"I see," the nurse said. "You've been calling me a lot. What did we talk about last time?"

"Something boring," Brennan chuckled. "I think it was the weather."

The nurse giggled and pulled out a rolling chair, wheeling her way towards Brennan.

Brennan had Olivia's long hair and it seemed to be making an attempt to blind him. Strands of his hair would float their way down to cover his eyes, but the nurse would always push them aside.

"You remind me of my little sister," she said.

For a moment Brennan felt the need to protest, but he snapped back to the realization that he wasn't himself anymore.

"Don't worry, I'm sure your family and friends will come around sometime," the nurse said.

But of course, she didn't know that Olivia's family were nothing more than strangers to him. He turned his head to face the ceiling and he put his forearm over his eyes to conceal the new onset of tears.

"I can guarantee you, they'll come." The nurse patted his shoulder and stood up as soon as her buzzer began to go off in her pocket. "Oh, looks like I have to tend to another patient. I'll check on you later." She walked out the door, but Brennan didn't dare to watch her leave again.

Where is everybody? His mind couldn't stop thinking of all the possible scenarios that could play out. Was someone, anyone, coming to see him? At first his heart fell at the thought of being alone, but that was soon replaced by fury.

"Bastards," he told himself. "They always leave me alone. Fuck my second chance." His mind went back to images of all the things he could use to bring him to death once again. "They can't make me stay if I don't want to." He laughed, at his own expense. Was he really willing to throw away his life once again? But after coming to that conclusion, he realized it wasn't his life to take. It was Olivia's.

As he was laughing at himself, Brennan heard the door creak and his eyes darted towards it. It gradually opened and a cute girl peeked her head through.

"Olivia," she said confused.

"Who are you?" Brennan called out.

The girl pushed her way into the room and Brennan finally had a good view of her. He checked her out from head to toe. She had short blonde hair with a perfect hourglass figure, and much to his amusement, she had the first couple of buttons of her shirt undone.

"It's me, Jessica," she stated.

"Oh, right." Brennan made a cocky voice like he was trying to impress her, but his facial expression said otherwise.

"You seem confused," she said. "Maybe you're just surprised to see me, of all people."

"I... well..."

"Don't worry, you don't have to say anything," she told him. Jessica walked towards him with a big smile on her face, but somehow, he got the impression that something was off. She rummaged through her purse and pulled out a tiny notebook. She lifted it up like it was a playing card and displayed it to him.

"What's that?" Brennan asked.

Jessica grinned and let out a short chuckle.

"Come on, don't play dumb," she said sarcastically.

Brennan gave a confused smile. "No, really. Tell me what it is?" he asked.

"You and I both know what this is." Her tone of voice changed into something much more sinister. "I just don't get why everyone's on your side," Jessica said.

"Me?" Brennan asked.

"Yes, dumbass."

Brennan's eyebrows raised and he wondered why someone would go from showing hospitality to hostility so fast. He felt the need to lash out, but this became a rare instance in his life when he decided to hold his tongue. Not for his sake, but for Olivia's. After all, she didn't come across as the type of person to talk down to others.

Facing a lock of response, Jessica gave Brennan a nasty face and smacked him. "It's your own damn fault!" she screamed.

"What is?" Brennan retorted.

"Because of you, my friends hate me. They always say, 'Oh, Jessica, you went too far this time. Look what you made her do.' It's not my fault you can't take a joke!"

Brennan rolled his eyes at her.

"So, they say you're the reason I tried to kill myself?"

After that, Jessica looked even more pissed, and she poked a finger at Brennan's chest.

"Don't mock me!"

"I'm not. I'm just trying to make sure I'm understanding everything correctly."

Jessica crossed her arms and pouted her lips, but not before throwing the tiny notebook at Brennan's face. The cover of it hit his nose and then fell down to his chest. When he picked it up and began skimming through the pages, all he saw were passages that started with dates written at the top of each page. Brennan realized he was reading a diary.

"I know all about your shit now," Jessica said, trying to sound tough.

"Are you trying to blackmail me?" To have a girl just jump into his life, with some sporadic personality and plan, confused him. Sure, Olivia may have known her, but to Brennan she was just some crazy girl.

"Your ass is mine for the next few months. Imagine if I posted this journal online!"

Brennan thought for a moment before coming to a conclusion. Olivia might have been a pushover, but seeing people like Jessica just made Brennan want to vomit. "Think about this," he said. "Everyone believes you drove me to suicide, and now you're trying to blackmail me? What if people found out you tried this?"

Brennan laughed a bit once he saw Jessica's eyes pop out in realization, and she sighed defeatedly.

"You're a bitch," she stated.

"Not as much as you." Brennan used his hand to signal her to scoot away but she didn't listen. He could feel his frustration growing, but managed to swallow it and maintain control. She might have been everything Brennan hated in a person, but she was the only person in Olivia's life that had talked to him, and so Brennan wiped his brow before telling her to take a seat. Jessica went over to the rolling chair the nurse had used and she pushed it next to Brennan's bed. "Look, let's at least try not to fight about this," Brennan told her. "We've both got ourselves in a bad situation."

Jessica kept her head down and stared at the floor while slowly spinning her chair left and right. She didn't respond for a while and the only sound in the room was the creak of the plastic wheels.

"This doesn't change anything," she said. "You're still just as pathetic as you always were."

"You know, I could say the same for you."

Jessica shot him a nasty look and made a short grunting sound.

"Why do I even talk to you?" she sighed sarcastically.

Brennan chuckled at her response as he came to a realization. His mind suddenly began calling himself a hypocrite. He always spent so much time conversing with people he hated, and for what?

"If you hate me so much, why do you talk to me?" He let a smile creep across his face, but Jessica didn't seem to be amused. She got up and slammed the door on her way out.

What a girl.

The next hour passed by uneventfully and Brennan found himself getting bored. He thought about Olivia and what she must be up to. Was she already adjusting to his life? The thought of her taking his place terrified him. What if she did something to screw him over? She did seem pretty frail to him.

She better not do anything stupid. Right now, his mind was dead set on finding her. Besides needing to return to his body, he didn't like the idea of having his reputation destroyed. After all, he had spent time showing others just how assertive he'd been, and Olivia was the complete opposite of that. Sure, if she were to stay in his body for long, people might see him as a nicer person, but "nice" might as well have been synonymous with "weak" in Brennan's eyes. If he was condemned to live the rest of his life, he certainly wouldn't want to spend it resolving problems that had been created for him. However, that thought had already etched itself in the back of his mind. Despite that, he dismissed each scenario where Olivia only added more to fuel to his problems. What if she was seen as too weak? What if his schoolmates took advantage of her? Worst of all, what if she learned too much about his personal life? Brennan decided he'd rather have some peace of mind instead. After that, he turned his memory back to the park with the children.

That sure seemed like something extraordinary, but there was a feeling deep inside his gut that made his heart ache at the thought of never seeing them again. Still, seeing Jessica might have been the best thing to happen to him since waking up. She seemed like the only real person here. The nurse was here just to do her job, while Haniel and the kids were some otherworldly beings. Jessica was just Jessica. She was a normal person, and even though she was abrasive, at least there was something to learn about Olivia's life through Jessica's hollow threats. But while Brennan's mind plagued him with loneliness, he opened Olivia's journal hoping that having something to read would ease the pain.

April 14

I've read somewhere online that keeping a journal can be pretty therapeutic. Maybe it'll keep my mind busy as I work things out. There's stuff I'd like to say and vent, but I only have myself to talk to. I guess it kinda sucks not to have anyone around. Every day I tend to walk around school with my earphones embedded into my skull, and today was no different. At least it wasn't different in that aspect. For some reason it felt better than normal. When I play my music, I don't hear anything else. It's like the chaos around me ceases and the day becomes bearable.

Also, I saw Mr. Jefferson out in the hall today. As always, he walked confidently to the teachers' lounge. He's such a great guy. Just hearing his lesson plans coming out of his mouth makes my heart race. He really knows what he's doing, and I love it. At least it, would be amazing, if Jessica didn't ruin everything.

April 15

Jessica is at it again. By now I've counted about 12 balls of paper thrown at me. A whole new record this time, but that doesn't matter anymore. I'd like to say things have gotten better just a tad, but I'd be lying...

Just another girl's pointless ramblings... Brennan closed the journal and sat back and yawned. He pushed it back under his pillow and folded his hands over his stomach. He picked up the remote beside his bed and debated whether or not he should call the nurse. But then again, what was the point? Just to talk to her? Talking to her wouldn't get him anywhere. Rather than summoning her, he pressed the button that would de-elevate his bed so that he could finally lie down. He dropped the remote and let it hang by its cord.

Pretty soon, I can get out of here. Brennan prayed that his time to leave the hospital would come soon, and then maybe he could figure out his whole situation. As to what there was to figure out, he didn't exactly know. Being thrown into a new life without any knowledge of his friends, family or acquaintances wasn't exactly a comforting thought. But Brennan knew that being here felt more like a prison than a safe space. The doors were electronically locked to keep patients in, and everywhere he went, one of the staff was required to follow him. Having all their eyes glued to him was one of the few things that made his heart thump. In his mind, a safe space was a quiet place. A place where he could retreat to without risk of running into anyone. *I have to leave.* He rolled over on his side and nuzzled his head into the pillow. Again, he was feeling dizzy, and the headaches were coming back. *Why'd you have to overdose, Olivia?* Brennan closed his eyes until sleep slowly draped over him like a blanket.

The next afternoon Brennan woke up feeling groggy and out of place. He gradually opened his eyes only to find that his vision was a mess. Everything around the room looked like a blurry array of little sprites dancing around. It took a while for his eyes to adjust, but when it did, he noticed a familiar girl sitting in the chair beside his bed. Jessica's head drooped as she sat still, and Brennan could hear the faint sound of snoring escape her throat. He leaned over and shook her shoulder until she jumped up. She stretched her arms out in the air and yawned.

"It's you again," Brennan said.

"Of course, it is," she said abruptly. Her eyes narrowed in on him and anger began to dawn on her face. "Just look at how shitty you are when you wake up."

Brennan meant to groan but it came out as a short laugh instead. "Why are you even here?" he asked.

"I don't have anyone else to hang out with, and trust me, I don't want to be here either. If my friends didn't backstab me, I would sure as shit hang out with them instead."

"They're still angry at you?"

Jessica sighed and played with her hair while she leaned back in the chair. "It's all because of you," she muttered.

Brennan could tell she was creating some distance between them due to the uneasiness she felt. With a sense of loneliness and anger, he wanted to just use Olivia's frail arms to grab Jessica's chair and pull her towards him. But that just wouldn't do. Surely Olivia wouldn't act that way.

"Could you come here for a moment," Brennan asked as sweetly as possible.

"Why should I?"

"I just need to talk to you."

"About what?" Jessica stuck her nose in the air as though she were royalty.

"About... everything..."

"I don't get what you mean."

"Just tell me everything that happened up until now." Bonding with Jessica wasn't something he really cared for, but learning more about Olivia's life was. After all, if people were to grow suspicious because of her sudden change in personality, it would attract more attention than he wanted. That type of attention would just bring more people closer to him, which would impede on his ability to slip away to Florida, unnoticed. "Let's just talk like normal people," Brennan said putting up an act. *Act like Olivia... Act like Olivia...*

"Yeah, sure." Jessica remained tense and it was obvious enough for Brennan to come to the conclusion that she meant to show it. He just made a disappointed face in return.

CHAPTER THREE

By now it had been about four days, and the nurses had finally gotten around to collecting all Olivia's things such as the worn-out toothbrush they gave her and Brennan's cell phone. The social workers went through their last set of questions – just the same queries to make sure she wasn't a danger to herself anymore. Lying in a pile by the bedside were the clothes they'd found Brennan in when he hanged himself, and when she saw them, her empathy kicked in. She imagined what Brennan must have gone through in his last moments.

"Why do you still have those?" she asked the nurse.

"We tend to keep all the patients' belongings until they're sent home. Clothing, electronics, wallets and everything else. Some of the patients we get here are homeless, and we don't want them to leave with nothing."

When Olivia was finally left alone in her room, she scooped them up and took off her hospital gown. She stared at her new body and wondered what she was going to do with it. She felt out of place looking at herself. His legs, arms and chest were bigger, which made her uncomfortable; she'd rather hide away in a small body than take up space in a bigger one, but rather than complaining some more, she set out to get into Brennan's old clothes. Olivia popped one leg through his sweatpants and then proceeded to do the same with the other limb. She tightly squeezed the strings of the pants and tied them into a knot.

First day out of here. Olivia took the black t-shirt and shoved her head through the top and then her arms out the sleeves. She looked back at the bed to make sure she hadn't forgotten anything, and sure enough, she almost missed Brennan's phone lying out in the open. She picked it up and pressed the button on the side. The screen glowed a bright blue and a blank four-digit passcode presented itself. What could his password have been? Olivia struck random numbers on the virtual keypad, but nothing happened, and eventually she was locked out of the device.

The phone's blue wallpaper was replaced by a red transparent overlay that read "five minutes." Olivia shook her head in frustration. With her need to leave as soon as possible, five minutes seemed more like five hours. She pushed the phone in her pocket and headed out the door. On the way out she still smelled the stench of urine and antiseptic, but the staff around her seemed livelier. Some of the nurses waved her goodbye as she passed, making her heart rise. Once she got to the lobby and sat down in the waiting area, she decided to slouch back and let her body feel the soft cushion of the chair. *What the hell am I going to do now?* She closed her eyes, but all she could hear was the sound of a young boy talking to his mother.

"How long are we going to wait?" he whined.

"Just hold on, your big sister will come back soon."

Olivia laughed a bit at their conversation, and pretty soon the presence of a young boy washed over her. She felt a cold sting on her skin, causing her to shudder.

What is that...? she asked herself, but the only thing out of the ordinary was the fleeting image of a young girl with white hair lurking around the corner. Olivia heard the voice of a young girl giggling and her eyelids shot open to scan the area. She got up and took a peek around the corner of the room, but all she found was a doll being cradled in the hands of a little boy. He had black hair and his pajamas had the same dark tint to them. He turned around to look at Olivia with a blank expression.

"Oh, I'm sorry to bother you," Olivia said. She got up and dismissed herself, but before she could turn away, the boy tugged at her pants.

"You're not Brennan," he said.

Suddenly Olivia's mind wasn't on auto pilot anymore. Once she heard his accusation, her attention had immediately shifted.

"What did you say?"

"You're not Brennan. I played with Brennan at the park. You *look* like him, but you're not him."

Olivia knelt down to his height and rubbed the top of his head. "Well, you must've known him well. What's your name?"

"Death," he quickly responded.

Considering her circumstances, Olivia wasn't the least bit surprised by his name. "Of course it is," she said sarcastically. "How'd you get here by the way?"

The boy turned his head away and faced the sliding door that led outside, but rather than saying anything, he just stared.

"Brennan, why are you talking to yourself?" Nora asked. She had come walking through the same set of doors, eagerly waiting for her brother.

Olivia got up from her kneeling position and stumbled a little. For some reason, Death gave off an aura that made her tense. She gave Nora an awkward laugh and smile, and when she turned around to face Death, he had vanished. With Nora staring at her, Olivia felt the need to come up with an excuse.

"It's nothing. Just doing a pep talk. Are we going home now?"

Nora nodded.

With a wave of her hand, Olivia decided to follow her. They went out into the parking lot. Nora pressed the button on her car keys and her vehicle lit up. It beeped, revealing its full form to be a silver minivan. They got in the car and with their headlights turned on, they pulled the car out of the parking lot. Olivia put her face up to the window to see the outside world. Was she really in Florida? Last time she checked it was the early start of May, but Nora had already turned the AC all the way up. Considering the heat, she must've been in Florida.

Once the car had finally made it onto the road, Nora picked up the pace. They zoomed past at forty miles per hour, which was enough to shake the bobble head on the dashboard.

"Well, you seem happy tonight," Nora said as she noticed Olivia's smile.

"I just can't wait to go home." Even though it wasn't her place to call home, Brennan's life was still a mystery to her. Maybe seeing Brennan's room, along with all his belongings, would give her a better idea. Not only that, but finally having some peace would be an added bonus.

Nora let out a tiny uncomfortable laugh. "You're technically not going home."

"What do you mean?"

"You'll be staying at my apartment!" Nora tried to punch Olivia on the arm, but accidentally swerved into the other lane, and when she regained control of the wheel, she made sure to stick to her side of the car.

"I'm not going home?" Olivia asked again. Why wouldn't she be taken to Brennan's house? Did someone not want her there? Olivia leaned her head against the window as disappointment washed over her.

"Don't worry about it," Nora said. "Everything will go back to normal soon."

"Is there anyone besides you that's waiting for me to come home?" Olivia asked. Sure, meeting new people seemed like a waste of time, but getting to know everyone might help her blend in.

"No, I'm sorry. But the two of us have always been doing fine. Am I right?"

For the first time since their initial encounter, Olivia saw Nora's lovely attitude change.

"I'm sorry. I didn't know what I was thinking." Olivia tried her best to perform damage control, but she could tell that pain still lingered in Nora's heart.

For a while the car ride continued in silence, but that silence still plagued them.

"You know, it's a good thing I still live in town," Nora said. "At least you'll be close to school."

"Oh, that's nice," Olivia replied sheepishly.

Nora slowed down the car to negotiate a turn, and they ended up going through a small neighborhood. As their headlights shone on the houses, it became apparent that everything was plainly similar. Just two-floored houses, colored light blue. The perfect home for an American sitcom.

"Is your apartment around here?" Olivia asked.

"Yeah. Don't you remember?"

"Um, I'm just feeling a bit off, since the... you know... I've been in the hospital," Olivia laughed nervously.

Nora stared at her. "But you used to try to come over all the time."

"Like I said, I'm just a little weirded out by everything."

"Are you okay?"

"I'm fine. Just let me get some rest, please." Olivia turned her head away to show that she wasn't willing to take any more questions, but Nora didn't look satisfied.

She took a left turn, and Olivia spotted a giant apartment complex. From there Nora pulled her car into the parking lot and stopped at her usual spot. "We'll get the rest of your things tomorrow," she said.

"How long will I be staying here?"

"Let's worry about that later. Come on." And with a sad expression, Nora walked towards the front door while using her hand to motion for Olivia to follow. Once they entered the lobby, the man sitting behind the front desk smiled and waved at them.

"Welcome back," he said before turning his attention to Olivia. "Who's he? Your boyfriend?"

Nora laughed at his assumption and placed her hand on Olivia's shoulders. "He may look older than he really is, but he's still my little brother."

The man blushed as he felt a little embarrassed. "Well, it's nice to meet you," he said to Olivia.

"Thank you," she said back.

After their brief encounter, Nora walked towards an elevator and waited for Olivia to follow, and when Olivia entered the lift, she found herself standing next to a keypad. She raised her hand to press a button, but hesitated.

"It's the third floor," Nora said, leaning over her.

Olivia pushed the button and the door closed. She felt herself rising up, and as always, the sensation made her body feel like it was being squished. However, once they stopped at the correct floor, all of that washed away.

Nora was the first to set foot outside and Olivia followed. The hallway glowed an orange tint and their footsteps could be heard smacking the wooden floor.

"You're stomping your feet again," Nora commented.

"Oh, I'm sorry."

"It's fine, it's just that I was hoping you'd stop doing that. It would always wake me up when we were kids." The word "kid" placed Olivia's mind in a position to think about her own childhood. Her dad had passed, and ever since, her mother just seemed like an empty shell. She hesitated for a bit, and Nora looked down to see her feet standing in place.

"Brennan? Is everything all right?" she asked.

"I honestly don't know what to tell you."

Nora rubbed the top of Olivia's head and smiled. "Just come inside, and we can talk like we always did."

They went in a straight line to a door at the far end of the hall. Nora pulled out her keys and twisted it in the knob. With that, the door flew open and together they went in.

"Welcome to your new home," Nora said. Once they entered the common room, Nora was already making herself comfortable on an old beat-up couch. "Remember this thing?" she asked. "We'd always jump on it and mom would yell at us." She giggled and beckoned for Olivia to come to her. "You can sleep here. If you need anything, my bedroom is right over there past the kitchen." Nora pointed to a door that seemed to be only a few paces away from the fridge. She stretched her arms out and yawned. "Well, I'm going to take a shower before I go to bed. Just make yourself comfortable here." And with that she got up and headed towards her room.

Olivia heard her rummaging through a dresser looking for clothes, and not too long after that, the sound of running water came.

Olivia took this moment to explore the apartment. At first, her curiosity peaked in the kitchen when she noticed the fridge. The metal door had a slew of pictures magnetically attached to it. Most of them were of Nora with a few other women at parties, but one photo stood out from the rest. Right there, in the middle of the fridge, was a photo of two young children playing with a ball. A colorful park on a bright sunny day dominated the background. One of the children was a little girl that didn't seem to be too much older than the boy she was playing with, and upon further inspection, Olivia could see that the young girl was Nora. Although her face seemed rounder and cuter back then, Olivia could tell from the other photos that Nora still retained some of those childish features. Her face may have been thinner, but those adorable brown eyes still remained. It also seemed like her fashion decisions hadn't changed much either. In the picture she was still wearing a shirt with a hoodie. She looked like she must've been twelve at the time. The boy had short black hair, and he wore miniature sweatpants and a t-shirt. From those clothes Olivia could immediately tell that the giddy boy was Brennan. He was smiling widely at his sister. His crooked baby teeth were exposing themselves just like in any other elementary school child, and off in the distance stood a man facing them. He wore a uniform for some company, and the name tag on his shirt read *Claufield.*

Is that his dad? Since his face was a blur, she used her imagination to fill in the blanks. She tried to imagine a man that had similar facial features to Brennan, but just thinking about a father figure brought her back to her childhood. She felt a stinging sensation in the back of her head, and after a short grimace, she turned her attention to the calendar hanging above the kitchen counter. It had images of puppies as decoration. *It's May twelfth.* By now Olivia would've been doing her final exams just before the start of summer break. Is Brennan's school doing the same thing? The next day would be a Thursday. Of course, she'd go to school, but from there, multiple compromises would have to be made. Surely people who she didn't know would recognize her. Brennan may have been a bit rough, but even rough people have friends, and those friends would be filled with questions.

Olivia laid her body down on the couch and hugged a pillow to her chest. She rolled over on her side and snuggled her face deeper into the cushion. *Tomorrow I'll figure things out,* she promised herself. She pulled her legs into the fetal position and closed her eyes. She rested until her mind went blank and her body went to sleep.

Brennan sat at the head of his bed while Jessica stayed at the other end with a pile of playing cards in between them.

"God, you're so dumb. Don't you know how to play?" Jessica sighed.

Brennan laughed and drew another card. "Shit, I'm over," he said.

Jessica reached over and smacked him on the arm while glaring. "You're not supposed to tell me, dumbass."

"Oh, alright."

Both of them revealed the deck they played with and laid it upon the bed sheet.

"I'm still over, but I'm closer to twenty-one," Jessica said with a triumphant attitude. She looked over at Brennan's cards to see what value they added up to. "What the hell is this? You're way over. It's almost thirty!"

Brennan gave a pathetic smile and raised his hands as if to say he surrendered. "Like I said, it's my first time playing," he pouted.

"But it's not that hard to count. Just get as close to twenty-one, without going over!" Jessica folded her arms over her chest and grunted. As always, she kept her mean persona, but she still took the time to keep Brennan company. She scooped up the cards and organized them into a stack. She slipped the cards back into their box and shoved it inside the pocket of her jeans. "How long are you going to be here?" she sighed, as she fell back onto the bed and stretched her arms out.

"Why? Do you want to see me at school?" When they'd first met, he'd sensed that Jessica was Olivia's enemy, but it seemed like that assumption was slowly turning blurry.

"I just don't want to keep coming here."

"Then why do you come here?"

Jessica sighed and rolled over to her side facing away from him. She picked at the blanket while using her arm as a makeshift pillow. "I just need to be with someone. Everyone else left me."

Brennan scratched his head in confusion. Surely she didn't mean that. People saying what they didn't mean always put him in a bad mood, but he made an exception for Jessica. Whether it was out of genuine curiosity, or he just needed to learn more about Olivia's life, he didn't know. "So, you felt the need to come here on your own?" he asked.

For a good few seconds Jessica hesitated to respond. "What are you getting at?" she asked angrily.

"I'm just trying to figure out what's going on here. I'm confused."

"You always were," Jessica muttered. She pushed his hand away and curled herself up into a ball as if she were a mouse hiding away.

"What's that supposed to mean?"

"Fuck off!" she snapped.

Brennan put his hands up in a pathetic defensive position due to both the unexpected hostility and randomness of her responses.

Jessica rolled on her back and stretched her body. She ended up letting out a tiny moan which was enough to make Brennan blush. "We need to get out of here," she said.

"Well, in case you haven't noticed, no one is coming for me."

Jessica sat up and rubbed her eyes. "I know," she said in a sad tone of voice.

"Maybe someone will come soon." Brennan wanted to think optimistically, but there didn't seem to be any hope left for him at all. Why didn't Olivia have any family members who cared enough to get her?

However, just as soon as that thought crossed his mind, a hunky man came walking through the door. He was clean-shaven, but had a drunken look in his eyes. "Olivia," he said.

Jessica turned to Brennan with a relieved smile. "Just in time," she said.

Brennan tried to force a smile of his own, but he was too busy examining the man. Who was he in relation to Olivia? His face was much firmer than hers and his eyes were green. What features could he have shared with her? Were they even related?

'It's time to go home," he said.

"Well, it's about time," said Jessica. She hopped off the bed like a rabbit and pulled Brennan's arm to follow her.

"Hold on," Brennan said.

"What's the matter? You've been here for almost a week. Let's just get out already!" Jessica exclaimed.

"Yeah, but –" Brennan couldn't find the right words to say.

Despite the man's pristine appearance, he still gave off an unpleasant feeling. It was the type of feeling that caused Brennan to revert to an animal-like state. The man stared at him intensely, almost as though he was looking *through* him rather than *at* him. He slowly walked forward, and Brennan could feel his presence consume him. Suddenly, Brennan didn't feel like himself anymore. He felt like a puppy being put up against a fully-grown adult male, and he felt that at any moment this man could dump him in his trunk.

"Come on, aren't you glad to see your stepfather?" the man said, grabbing Brennan's wrist.

Brennan tried to pull back, but the man just gripped him even tighter. He forced a fake smile while gritting his teeth, and forcefully pulled Brennan closer before they both walked out the door.

Jessica followed alongside them.

"Wait, what about all my stuff?" Brennan asked, trying to buy time. At this point, anything that would keep him from being alone with this man would be a blessing.

"Don't worry, everything's been taken care of. I'm just here to pick you up."

"No, wait," Brennan pleaded.

"What?" the man snapped. He tightened his grip to the point where it could leave a mark, and both Brennan and Jessica were caught off guard. "Sorry," he said, trying to regain his composure. "I just want you to come home. Your mother and I miss you."

"Hey, sir..." Jessica tried to reason with him, but she was cut off. Even compared to her horrid personality, this man was too much.

"Call me Mr. Benning," he said.

"Yes, sorry."

Brennan was baffled by Jessica's reaction. What happened to that tough girl that raised hell for everybody? Why was she suddenly backing down?

"I need a ride home," Jessica stuttered.

"Just call your parents," Mr. Benning said.

And for the first time since they'd met, Brennan noticed an ounce of empathy on Jessica's face.

Once they entered the lobby, the nurse headed their way and handed Olivia's old clothes to Brennan. Mr. Benning eyed him up and down just before Brennan went into the bathroom. He shut the door and then slipped out of his hospital gown. The mirror showed Brennan everything about his new body. From the arms, thighs, and chest, everything was different, and Brennan felt like a pervert for staring. He slid his slender legs into the skinny jeans before putting on a pink shirt. Afterwards, he popped the gray hoodie on and took one last look in the mirror. *Just like my sister.*

Olivia seemed to have an uncanny resemblance to Nora's sense of fashion, and the memory almost forced tears out of him. Suddenly his mind was traversing through all the moments he'd spent with Nora. From playing hide-and-seek, to hiding away from their mother, everything surfaced. When would be the next time he'd see her?

Mr. Benning led Brennan to an old run-down truck awaiting them in the parking lot. When he finally let go of his hand, Mr. Benning went to the driver's side of the truck and hopped in. "Well, get inside," he told Brennan.

Against his better judgement, Brennan forced himself to go in and the lock on the doors instantly snapped shut. They made a popping sound, and Brennan's whole body jumped at the realization that he couldn't escape. His new stepfather started the ignition, and in a matter of seconds they were out of the parking lot.

They drove down the road until they came to a traffic light which was flashing red.

"You know, me and you mother missed you," Mr. Benning said.

"Thanks," Brennan said as more of a question.

"Yes, we definitely did." He slowly reached his hand over to the passenger's seat with the intention to hold onto Brennan, but this time, rather than a tight grip, Mr. Benning gently caressed his hand. Brennan quickly acted on the urge to pull away and snuggled against the door.

"Don't be scared," Mr. Benning said, like a snake waiting in a bush. He stared at Brennan like he was ready to pounce on him.

The feeling of being dominated resurfaced in Brennan, even though he had spent most of his life burying it away.

"Don't worry about anything." The deceptive tone of Mr. Benning's voice was interrupted by the sound of a car honking their horn.

Brennan wanted to roll down his window and wave at them to come and save him.

"Oh, the light's green," Mr. Benning muttered before stepping on the gas.

Once that little glimmer of hope passed, Brennan's heart died a little. He pulled every part of his body closer, as though they formed a protective shell.

"You always gave me that look when you were scared," Mr. Benning taunted. "I know you want to go back to school and see your friends again, but why don't you just stay home with me for a while?"

"Don't you have work to do?" Brennan tried to come up with an excuse to create some distance between them, but he ultimately failed.

Mr. Benning sighed and loosened up his shoulders. "Don't tell your mom this, but I got fired from my job."

"Why?" Brennan asked.

"It's nothing you should worry about. At least it means we get to spend more time with each other."

In any normal circumstances this would be a pleasant surprise for a kid; who wouldn't like to spend more time with their father? But there was still something off about this man. His words felt like they could cut through his skin and move around his entire body. There was a certain atmosphere to him that could make any child cry, and that's when Mr. Benning placed a hand on Brennan's knee. He gently moved it up and down, forcing Brennan give up his fear in favor of courage.

"Stop it," he demanded.

"You shouldn't talk to your father that way," Mr. Benning growled.

"You shouldn't touch your daughter that way," Brennan said, gritting his teeth.

From there, Mr. Benning placed a firm grip on Olivia's skinny thighs.

Brennan felt his ginormous hands leaving a bruise. "I said stop! It fucking hurts! Stop!"

"You watch your damn mouth!" Mr. Benning yelled.

Brennan felt the fighter in him want to make a grand entrance, and so he bent over and bit Mr. Benning's finger as hard as he could.

The man wailed as he tried to wiggle out of Brennan's teeth, but he could only get away when his blood was able to be used as lubricant. He pulled his hand back and quickly slammed on the brakes. He set the car to *Park* as he delicately rubbed his finger. "You fucking bitch! You fucking whore!" He wound up his right arm and struck Brennan with full force right in his eye.

The force was enough to smash the back of his head against the window. Brennan leaned back and raised his foot to kick Mr. Benning straight in the nose, and as he bled, Brennan unlocked his door and rolled out of the car. The road they were on was next to nothing but farms and open fields. Brennan tried to burst into a sprint, but he could already feel the limitations of Olivia's body. He wasn't as fast as he used to be, and he barely had enough strength to hoist his body over the fence. However, once he did, it was a clear path to freedom. He trudged forward and only looked back to raise his middle finger at Olivia's stepfather.

Brennan picked up a run again, straight towards a house on the outskirts of the farm. He marched his way through crops and cow waste until he got to his safe haven. By then Brennan's clothes were sticking to his body by the sweat that poured through his skin. He pounded his fist on the front door and a large man trundled his way over, dressed in a shirt that showed off his big gut and pants that were larger than his massive legs. He pulled open the door.

"What do you want?" he asked groggily.

"I need to get inside and use your phone."

"What for?"

"I just ran well over a mile to get away from my stepdad."

"You're a runaway?" he asked.

Brennan stopped for a moment to think.

"Yeah, I guess so," he sighed. "Just let me make a call so I can get home safely."

"Fine, but be quick. I don't want to get in any trouble. The phone is in the kitchen."

Brennan hastily walked in and towards the landline affixed to the wall.

The farmer sat down on his sofa and cracked open a couple of beers as he watched the television. After chugging each drink down he crushed the can in his hands. He yelled at the screen and threw a can at it.

After that, the sound of nails scratching against wood could be heard coming closer, and sure enough, a dog came walking around the corner to inspect the noise. She was a tiny beagle, and Brennan guessed it must still be a puppy.

"Don't worry, little girl," the man said to his dog. She raced towards him and jumped on the couch. She curled up and nestled in his lap. He gently petted her as he reached for another drink, and during all this time, Brennan had been holding the phone to his ear wondering who to call. He could phone the police, but he barely even knew his new name and he had no idea where he was, but then he thought of the time he exchanged phone numbers with Olivia.

She must have my phone.

He took a leap of faith and dialed his own phone number, hoping that by chance Olivia would be in possession of it, and for a few seconds he stood listening to the phone buzz. Eventually, someone answered, and Brennan heard his own voice speaking to him.

"Hello?" it said.

"Olivia, is that you?" Brennan asked quickly.

"Oh my god, Brennan?"

"It's me. It's me!" he happily repeated.

"Where are you? Are you at my house right now?"

"No, your creepy stepdad just tried to make a move on me. I jumped out of the car the moment I could."

"Oh," Olivia's voice trailed off.

"Listen, I'm not going to deal with that. I'm calling the cops."

"Wait, no!" Olivia screamed. "He's still my dad," she pleaded.

"He's a predator!" Brennan yelled back.

"But my mom still loves him. I don't want any more trouble for my family."

"I don't care. I'm not dealing with this." Brennan could hear Olivia's voice shake on her end. "Listen to me. He has to go," Brennan told her.

"This is my life you're changing! Mine! Remember that!"

There was a brief pause between the two of them and the phone line went silent.

"You're still living my life. Don't mess it up," Olivia said. Brennan could hear the faint sound of sobbing coming from her end.

"I'm pretty sure I'd be doing you a favor." His voice began to show signs of aggression.

"Let me deal with it for now," she begged.

"You need to grow a damn backbone," he lectured. "You just let people walk all over you."

"What makes you say that?"

"I read your journal. Jessica gave it to me – I mean *you* – and..." Brennan stopped short and realized he had been talking without thinking. "Ah, just forget what I said."

"Wait, why are you with her?" Rather than turning to pure rage, Olivia's voice turned to that of confusion. "She actually took the time to visit you, and you read my diary which she gave you?"

"Well, first off," said Brennan, "I read your diary because I wanted to get an idea of what *I* was getting myself into. And about Jessica... She's been confusing me. From what I get, she bullied you?"

"Yeah, that's why I don't know why she'd be with you."

"From what it looks like, I think she just feels guilty."

"You're insane to spend time with her."

"I don't care, I need to use her to get familiar with your life."

"No, wait!"

"Wait, what? What else am I going to do? Just listen to you tell me a summary of your life and then forget it the next day!?" Brennan yelled.

"But I'm not like that! As much as I hate her, I'm not like that! Can't you at least *pretend* to be me?"

Brennan clenched his fist. He just couldn't catch a break. From being resurrected to being berated, he just couldn't handle it. He wanted to keep his words to himself, but they came bursting out. "Well, listen to me, you little piece of shit! I've been stuck in a fucking hospital, and the moment I get out, it's just another version of Hell! You don't know what I've been going through!"

"Really?" Olivia said sarcastically. "You're living my life! *Of course* I know!"

Brennan grunted in frustration. "Okay, fine. You win."

"Brennan, you really need to learn how to show compassion."

"I do have compassion," he said. "But I just want to fix our little dilemma so I can go back to my old body and finish what I started."

"You're honestly not going to do that, right? Everyone here loves you. Your sister has shown me so much support, and your teacher does the same thing."

"You obviously don't know the rest of my life," he said through gritted teeth. "You're an idiot, you know that?"

Olivia thought for a moment. "Let's just figure out what to do next," she sighed, changing the subject. "Where are you right now?"

"Considering the cold, and your Space Needle shirt, I'm guessing this is Washington."

"Well, your deductive skills are excellent," she laughed, trying to make light of the situation.

"The shitty thing is I live in Florida. How am I supposed to get to you?"

"I'm sure we'll figure something out. By the way, if we do find each other, what do we do next?"

For a moment the phone line went silent.

"Like you said, we'll figure something out," Brennan told her.

"Hey, are you done in there?" the farmer yelled.

"Almost!" Brennan yelled back.

"Brennan, who is that?" Olivia asked.

"Remember when I said I ran away from your stepdad? Well, this is where I found myself, and I have no idea where I'll stay for now. I'm not going back to him."

"I... I don't know what to tell you. Oh fuck."

This was the first time Brennan had heard her utter a cuss, and it was oddly satisfying. "Oh shit! Oh shit, I don't know," she continued.

Brennan noticed the onset of panic setting into Olivia.

"Hey, calm down," he said. "If you want me to act like you, then you should at least try to act like me."

"What? What about *you*? You're nothing like me!"

"Don't take offense at this, but... you need to be more assertive."

"Oh you –" Olivia stopped short and hesitated on lecturing him. "Fine, I'll do my best. Anyways, what are you going to do?"

"I've always made compromises, and I'll do it again." Brennan said. "I'll find a way to call you later. Don't screw things up for me."

"Wait. I just –"

But before she could finish, Brennan hung up the phone and left with the reality that he had no clue where to go. Here he was at about 9 p.m. with some farmer getting drunk out of his mind.

Brennan tiptoed out of the kitchen and peeked around the corner. The farmer had already drunk himself to sleep and the dog was the only one keeping an eye on things, so Brennan casually walked outside without attracting any attention.

Now, he had to find a new place to lie low.

This time, running through the farm seemed to be much easier, much quicker. By the time Brennan was back on the road, the air began to freeze him. His whole body shuddered. He started to rub his arms with his hands with enough friction to create a fire. His skin was beginning to show goosebumps, and so he began jogging, despite feeling tired. He couldn't remember exactly where he and Mr. Benning were driving, so he picked a direction at random, hoping that it would lead him back into town.

However, the further he walked, the more trees and farmland he saw. It wasn't until a car's headlights came into view that hope began to return to him. He'd never hitch-hiked before, so this was a new experience. *God. I know you exist now, so please make sure this driver isn't a serial killer.* The closer the vehicle approached, the more of it Brennan could see. It was a rusty truck that only had seats for two people. Brennan stuck out his thumb, just like he had seen people do in movies.

When the driver stopped, he was relieved to see Jessica behind the wheel.

"Jessica?"

"What the hell? Why are you out here all by yourself?" she asked.

"I just ran away from my stepdad."

Jessica averted her gaze towards the steering wheel.

"By the way, Jessical, I thought you needed a ride home. Why the hell are you driving a truck when you said you needed a ride?"

"I just needed an excuse to spend more time with you."

"Whatever, I'm not complaining." Without another word, Brennan went around to the passenger's side, and pulled open the door to hop in.

Chapter Four

The wheels of the truck crunched over the road as Brennan sat in the passenger's seat. Coming across Jessica had made things turn over for the better. Who knew that as he was wandering by the roadside, Jessica would just happen to be driving home? By the time she found him, Brennan was like an orphaned child suffering in the cold. Her heated truck in such cold weather seemed like a gift from God, and by now Brennan was slightly bruised, but as always, he soldiered on and dealt with the pain.

"So, you had to run away?" Jessica asked.

"And why did you decide to help me?" Brennan prodded.

"Look, you don't need to keep pestering me. I just gave you a free ride. If anything, you should be grateful."

"Trust me, I am."

"Well, what are you going to do now?"

"Mr. Ben– I mean, my stepdad – tried to make a move on me, so I'm definitely not going home."

"Yeah, I too got a bad feeling from him." Jessica slightly craned her neck to the side and gave Brennan a sympathetic look.

"Yup, your gut was right." Brennan tilted his seat back and put his feet on the dashboard.

"Hey!" Jessica slapped his shin as she yelled at him to put his feet down, but he declined her demand. "God," she sighed. "What happened to you?"

"What do you mean?"

"It's just that... You didn't seem to be that big of a prick before."

"Oh, and what about you? Weren't you the one who bullied me into submission?" Brennan asked.

"Yeah, you're right, but you don't need to keep reminding me."

"What, do you think you can just forget about that?"

"No, but..." Jessica grunted in frustration.

It became clear that Brennan had shoved her into a corner and she had nowhere else to turn to.

"Alright, maybe it's the guilt, or maybe I actually don't have a heart made of stone, but I'm trying to fix things here."

"Are you sure? No one I've ever met has swallowed their pride." Brennan laid his head against the window and let his eyes look outside as the car passed by hundreds of trees and farmland.

Jessica heavily exhaled out to calm her nerves. "Trust me, when people want to help you, let them help you. Don't push them away." She seemed to be getting more frustrated by the minute, but Brennan kept a cool head and a firm belief that he was right.

"Oh, and I supposed you're used to getting help," he retorted.

"What's that supposed to mean?"

"I know people like you. People like you get love and attention from everybody. They don't know what it feels like to be left alone!" Brennan raised his voice at her and Jessica almost let that drive her off the road.

"What are you talking about?" she yelled. "First off, I'll admit I did bully you, but that's all you knew me as. A fucking bully. You never knew anything else. Don't start assuming shit you don't know!"

Jessica's tirade was enough to put a dent into Brennan's horrible demeanor. So now he shut his mouth and put his head down. After a pause he asked, "So, you're telling me there's more to you than being a bastard?"

Jessica closed her eyes for a brief moment and exhaled a puff of air. "Yes, that's what I'm trying to say." This time she spoke more calmly. "I'll admit, I do feel guilty for bullying you, and I know guilt isn't enough to earn forgiveness, but just let me try to make things right," she begged. "By the way, what happened to you? I remember picking on this sweet innocent girl, but look at you now."

"I just decided a change was needed," Brennan told her.

"Well, in my personal experience, change can also be bad, and I'd say you're falling on the bad side."

"What? You don't know what it's like to be pushed around."

"Like I said, there's more to a person than what you see. You can stand up for yourself, but let me tell you – it can get to a point where you just turn into something you hate, and that's not good for anybody." Jessica's face seemed distant as she stared more intensely at the road in front of her.

To Brennan it seemed as though their little argument had taken its toll, and he also found himself feeling exhausted. He tried to drift off to sleep, but Jessica snapped him awake.

"No, don't got go sleep. Not yet anyway," she said. "Once I we get to my house you can nod off, but I want to talk to you some more."

"Fuck off," Brennan raised his middle finger before crossing his arms and finally shutting his eyes.

"Hey!" Jessica snapped. She slapped Brennan's shin in order to keep him from dozing off.

"Stop bothering me! What, are you going to get lonely?"

"No, I just don't want to be left alone with my thoughts."

"Oh, really?" Brennan asked.

"No, I don't."

"And what are you thinking about?"

"Look, that's not important, so –"

"Well, you want me to keep talking to you, so why don't you answer my questions?" As usual, Brennan started to push the boundary and get under Jessica's skin, and for a moment she didn't respond.

"I'll just say, I don't like being alone. I'd prefer to be with other people."

"That's ironic, considering how you tend to drive others away."

"I know I should feel guilty, and I do, but –"

"But what?" Brennan interrupted. "Do you think being sorry changes anything? The thought that you feel guilty doesn't take back what you've done."

"I know it doesn't, but can't you understand what I'm getting at?" Jessica's tone of voice indicated begging, and Brennan could've sworn he sensed the oncoming fall of tears. "Don't think for a moment I can just forget what I said or what I did. I know I don't deserve much sympathy, but Goddammit, where's the 'nice Olivia'? Did I ruin you that much?" This time her voice broke apart as the tears started to stream down the sides of her face, and despite the pitiful sight, Brennan wasn't moved at all.

"Are you apologizing for me or for yourself?" Brennan asked.

"Both," Jessica quietly cried.

"Yeah, sure you are."

"I know you have a bigger heart than me. Are you just changing into an asshole for my sake? I've seen you show compassion before. You used my phone to text that boy. Brennan was his name, right?"

Brennan closed his eyes and bowed his head. He exhaled some air to let off steam and then opened his eyes when he was ready to see things from a clearer perspective.

"So, you want sympathy from me now, is that it?" he asked.

"I just want you to listen to me."

"Fine."

"Have you ever had the feeling that everything around you is crashing and breaking apart, even yourself?"

"Well, considering what I did, yes," Brennan said. "Of course, I've felt that."

"Well, now that everyone is shutting me out, I can see how wrong I've been." Jessica pulled over on the side of the road and set the car to *Park*. She gripped the wheel tightly and slowly jammed her head into the center of it. Her body jerked forwards and backwards due to her crying. "Just look at the mess I've made!" she sobbed hysterically. "I almost got you killed, and I've been treating everyone like shit. Even the two friends that stayed by my side, I've treated them like shit." Jessica cried harder into the wheel but Brennan was hesitant to comfort her. "I'm sorry! I'm *so* sorry!" she cried. "Why am I the way I am? Why?" She quickly lifted her head and exposed her teary eyes to Brennan. He could tell that she was looking for an answer that neither of them knew. Her lip was quivering, and her sad eyes seemed to pierce into Brennan's mind.

"Quit crying and get us home," he said, keeping his distance. "We can talk about this later, not now." He maintained a commanding tone, and Jessica started the car again.

"My parents are in Vegas for a couple of weeks. Just stay with me for a while, okay?" Jessica took a moment to look at Brennan and he nodded.

"As long as I get to stay away from my stepdad."

"And Olivia," she said, turning to him.

For a moment Brennan didn't react to that name. It wasn't until Jessica said it again, that he realized she was talking to him.

"What?"

"Please go back to your old self."

"My old self? That cowardly girl I used to be?"

"No, not that. I mean, being a caring person that gives people a second chance. Being kind doesn't necessarily mean you're a coward. It just shows that you have a heart and if anything, you're still just as strong."

"I'm not going to let people walk all over me again," Brennan argued.

"Trust me, you don't have to. There's a difference between being a suck-up and doing what's right."

"Oh yeah? And what's the difference?" Brennan asked.

"Well... A suck-up is just looking for approval from others, even at the expense of their own dignity. When you do the right thing, you just do it because you know it's what should be done. On the plus side, it's courteous." Jessica smiled as her final tear dripped from her eye.

For the most part, the rest of the drive went by quietly. Brennan was mentally exhausted from their long talk, and he was ready to take a rest. Despite it being a school night, they both agreed on spending the night together, but once they were just a couple of blocks from her house, she came to a realization.

"Your parents will be wondering where you are. Shit, what are we going to do?"

"Why not just call them?" Brennan said.

"I hope you're joking. After escaping from your dad, I doubt they'll be happy to talk."

"You mean *stepdad*... And I don't know what else to do. Unless you're willing to run the risk of being charged with harboring a runaway."

"Well, I guess you better convince your parents to let you stay with me, otherwise I'm driving you home."

Brennan pulled out Olivia's phone, but then stopped for a minute. "I still don't know the password to my phone," he said defeatedly.

"Fine, take mine." Jessica took her attention off the road and pulled out her mobile. She turned it on and almost crashed the car off the side of the road.

"Be careful!" Brennan yelled. "Let me get it."

Jessica immediately dropped her phone on the floor but continued to hold the steering wheel with both hands. She focused her attention on driving as Brennan picked it up.

"The password is 3, 1, 2, 6, 5," she told him.

Brennan entered the digits and saw a background of Jessica with her two friends sitting in a cart on a Ferris wheel. They were each smiling at the camera as though nothing could separate them. For a moment Brennan thought he saw true love and compassion in Jessica's eyes. She sat in the middle of her two companions and put her arms around their shoulders.

"That's a cute picture," he said.

"What?" Jessica quickly glanced back at her phone and realized what he was getting at. "Yeah, that was a while back. Hopefully after some time they'll forgive me, and we can go back to being friends."

"Yeah, hopefully." Brennan began to swipe through each screen until he found an icon that would lead him to the keypad, but then he hesitated. Realizing that he didn't have the number he needed, he decided to phone Olivia instead, and so he called his own number.

The time zone difference was in effect, and so Olivia's sleep was interrupted at the sound of Brennan's ringtone. The moment he called his phone, a rock song played, but not for long. Despite her grogginess, Olivia made sure to answer as soon as possible. When she did, she lifted the mobile to her ear.

"Brennan?" she whispered.

"I need your mom's phone number," he whispered.

"Why?"

"Keep your voice down. I'm with Jessica, and for all she knows, I'm just mumbling into her phone, talking to your mom."

"What the hell are you doing?" Olivia pestered. "Why are you still with her?"

"Well, in case I didn't tell you before, your stepdad is a pervert. There's no way I'm staying anywhere near him. Jessica is like a sweet puppy compared to him."

"You don't know anything about her, or how she treated me."

"I know, but lately she's been telling me some things about your 'relationship'. I'm getting the idea, but she's still the best option I have right now."

Olivia sighed and muttered something under her breath. "Okay, okay, fine."

"I know you're stressed, but I promise, I'll figure things out."

"That's what you've been saying so far, but nothing's changed."

"Hey, this just takes time. I'm going to fix things, trust me on that."

"Alright, but have you thought about how we should meet up?" she asked.

The line went silent, and Olivia knew that neither one of them had an answer.

"I'll take a really long road trip."

"So that's it then? Just a road trip? Not only that, but you're spending time with Jessica," Olivia mumbled through the phone.

"I know you have a problem with her but –"

"You don't have to say anything else. I just can't shake off the fact that she wants to be around you…" Olivia's voice trailed off.

"I know things seem strange, but like I said, I'll fix everything. You just have to do what I say. Now, I need that phone number."

"Fine." After that Olivia gave away her mother's phone number and went back to sleep.

By now Jessica had reached her neighborhood and slowed the car right down to a good twenty-five miles per hour. All the houses stood in line with each other and were covered in white paint, making them look more like a barracks rather than a neighborhood. She turned around the corner and parked her car in the driveway of a two-floor house.

"We're here. Why were you talking so quietly to your mom?" she asked, turning to Brennan.

"She said my stepdad was sleeping. Did you catch any of what we said?"

"No, and I'm not going to ask. I've been nosey about your life lately." Jessica showed an apologetic attitude again, before stepping out of the vehicle. She marched her way towards the garage door. Off to the side was a keypad that she flipped open to enter a code. After a few stabs at the number keys, the garage door lifted itself up while creaking under its heavy weight.

"You go on ahead," Brennan called out to Jessica.

She turned around and gave him a confused look. "Why? Don't you want to come inside?"

"I will, I just need to call someone else. And like you said, you've been too nosey. Some privacy will do me good."

Jessica nodded her head and quietly entered the house. Realizing that he couldn't just pretend to talk to Olivia's mom, he racked his brain for her number. Brennan felt like an idiot for not asking for a pen to write it down. Once he remembered it, he anxiously waited for Olivia's mom to answer the phone. If he could just spend the night there without anyone worrying about his whereabouts, he would. But surely without any notification, Olivia's parents would hunt him down.

"Hey, Mom," Brennan said once his call was answered. "I'm going to stay at a friend's house."

"What? First your father comes home without you, and it's because you're trying to leave us again?"

"Listen to me, I don't want anything to do with you right now. I'm staying here!"

Despite her sweet voice, it seemed that Brennan's insulting assertiveness made her turn to sorrow. "Don't talk to me like that," she said sadly.

"Like I said, I'm not coming home. I'm going to stay with a friend tonight."

"Please, just come home."

"You're expecting me to go home to you? You didn't even visit me when I was in the hospital! Doesn't seem like you care that much."

The line went quiet, and Brennan heard a bit of crying coming from Olivia's mother.

"Well, that's..." She didn't finish her sentence, and even though Brennan had a stone-cold heart, guilt forced it to beat again.

"I know this may be tough," he said quietly, "but I need this."

"Fine, but promise me you'll come home tomorrow."

"I will. I promise."

Even though Brennan clearly got his message across, he still felt a little ugly for his methods, and he wondered why. Never before had intimidation and manipulation felt so bad to him. So why now?

"Well, what did she say?" Jessica asked once he got inside.

"I convinced her to say 'yes.'"

"How'd you do that?"

"Don't even think about it," Brennan told her.

Once they settled in, Brennan felt like he'd entered a rabbit hole. A warm feeling had engulfed the entire house, and the furniture, combined with the fireplace, added a lot to the atmosphere.

"Hey, could you take your shoes off?" Jessica asked politely.

Brennan took one look at her before reaching down and untying his laces. Then he rudely kicked both shoes off, and they flew across the room until they smacked against the front door. Even though he knew it was wrong, he just felt the need to be himself again. The unwavering guilt was getting to him, and he wasn't used to dealing with his emotions.

"Nice," Jessica sighed. She bent over to pick them up and quickly tossed them into the garage. "Well, this house is ours for a week."

"I'm only staying for the night," Brennan said.

"What? Why?"

"Sorry, but that's the best I could get out of my mom."

Jessica slumped her shoulders back and laid on the couch. "Damn," she said.

"Hey, if you're willing to let me come over another time, I'd be glad to. Anything to get away from my stepdad."

At this proposal, Jessica's body sat up straight with amazing posture. "Yes, that'd be great!" For a moment her happy demeanor wiped away Brennan's memory that she was once a bully. "Wow, this will be great." She leaned over to Brennan and gave him a big, unwanted hug. She squeezed him so tightly that he felt the need to push her away.

"Hey, just because I'd rather stay here doesn't mean I like you. I just hate my dad more than you."

Jessica's smile quickly faded into a frown, and she crossed her arms over her chest. "Why do you have to ruin it like that?" she muttered.

After the two of them were left in silence, the quiet, combined with Brennan's angry expression, had set them up for an awkward situation.

"So," Jessica said trying to break the silence. "You mentioned a trip earlier to your friend."

"Oh yeah, about that. It's sure to be a long trip, but I can promise you it's necessary."

"Can I come along?" Jessica asked eagerly.

"Well, considering that I don't have a license, I'd say yes."

"Great!" Jessica clapped her hands together like a giddy school-girl. "Where are we going?"

"Florida," Brennan muttered.

"That... that changes things," Jessica stuttered. "How the hell are we going to get that far? It's literally across the country!"

"Relax. You said your parents would be gone for a week, and running away seems to be my specialty. The way I see it, we have a week to get over there."

"And then what? How long will we be staying there? Did you even think about the time it would take to get back?"

Brennan had completely forgotten that this wouldn't be a one-way trip. "Just give me some time to think about it," he said. "I just really need to see a friend."

"Who? That boyfriend of yours? What's his name? Brennan?"

"He's not my boyfriend!" Brennan yelled.

"Oh?"

"I don't even like boys." Suddenly Brennan stopped and became aware that he wasn't speaking for himself.

"Are you telling me you're gay?" Jessica asked confused.

"No, no, I'm not."

"Don't worry, I won't tell anyone." Jessica raised her hands up and blushed.

"But I'm not – Oh, never mind." Brennan stopped himself when he recognized that there was no damage control he could pursue.

"It's fine," Jessica laughed and patted the top of his head, even though Brennan found no amusement in it.

"Just let me plan everything for now," he sighed.

"Actually, I need help with something," Jessica said.

"Oh shit, what is it now?"

"Well, Mr. Jefferson told us to write a poem to read to the class and it's due tomorrow." She nervously laughed at herself as she tried to create some distance.

"But I don't know how to write," Brennan said.

"Don't play dumb. Mr. Jefferson loves your writing. You're the best writer we have!"

"Shit," Brennan muttered. Now he needed to become a great writer too. The only reason he ever took a creative writing class was for the credit he needed to graduate. "Alright, I'll see what I can do."

After that, Jessica ran up the steps in search of her backpack.

Chapter Five

Olivia was still exhausted from Nora waking her up to drive to school. She was sitting in a closed bathroom stall, pondering her thoughts. What was she going to do with Brennan? Their talk about her stepfather had revealed so much about each other, yet at the same time she knew so little about *his* life. Olivia felt that the whole conversation remained one-sided, since she was being left in the dark with no one else to turn to.

Even her first day of school had been one big disaster after another. She barely knew any of her teachers, and the layout of the building was completely foreign to her. Despite this, she pressed forward and got out of the stall. She slowly opened the bathroom door, but paused. What was going through her head? Why was she having second thoughts now?

"I can get through this," she muttered.

Luckily for her, Brennan had left his class schedule in his backpack. The only problem was locating exactly where those classes were. She held the schedule in front of her face and stared at the first set of text written at the very top. *English, Mr. Heart 23B 9:00-10:00.*

So that's the room number? Considering that the time said nine o'clock, Olivia knew that meant her arrival time was long overdue. She followed the purple signs on the walls that pointed to each wing of the school, and in a matter of minutes she reached a room with the letters "Twenty-three B". Finally, she got to her destination. She moved her hand towards the door handle and made an entrance into the classroom.

Mr. Heart stopped lecturing and turned his attention towards her. "You're late," he said.

"I... I'm sorry. I just..." Olivia couldn't find the right words to say.

"Just go ahead and take a seat," Mr. Heart told her.

Olivia took in the classroom, and sure enough it looked almost identical to Mr. Jefferson's class – just plain white walls with posters of writers plastered against them. In the back were four empty seats, each waiting for Olivia to make her choice. She went to the one closest to the window, and prayed that the teacher didn't have an assigned seating chart. She got right on the chair and felt at home being next to the window, but from then on, she received curious looks from the students around her. Some expressed disappointment and resentment at the sight of her, but Olivia tried her best to ignore them and keep her eyes on the teacher.

"Now, since it's the end of the year, I'm going to be a little more lenient, and for your last grade I'll be giving you an assignment in creative writing."

There was a mixture of grunts and cheers from the students.

"But we're still going to learn," Mr. Heart told them. "Let's take a look at some of the most famous authors." He rummaged through the surface of his cluttered desk until he located a remote. He pressed a button and an image appeared on the white screen in front of the class.

"Why can't we just start writing?" one student complained. He crossed his arms over his chest and laughed as though he'd told a great joke.

However, no one joined in the laughter.

"We're going to take a look at these authors for inspiration," Mr. Heart said through gritted teeth. "Remember, a writer who doesn't read is like a film director who doesn't watch films. We read and we learn."

From then it became clear that Mr. Heart was presenting a slideshow that depicted different classical writers, along with bits of their work. He would slowly go through each author and give small talk about their literature before continuing to the next slide, but he gave special attention to Edgar Allen Poe.

"Anyone know this man?" he asked, looking around the room. "Come on, guys, he's my favorite author. He's known for writing those dark stories you all love to read."

"Is it H.P. Lovecraft?" a student called out.

"No, but good guess. Would anyone else like to try?" Mr. Heart seemed to show more interest in the subject than his students, and for a moment he felt that they were hopelessly lost.

"That's Edgar Allen Poe," Olivia said out loud.

Mr. Heart smiled at her and nodded his head.

"I see that today you decided to participate," he said. "I assume you've read some of his work?"

"Yes, but –"

And did you like it?" he interrupted.

"Actually, no," Olivia stated.

"Oh, but why?"

"I just think his attempts at humor and romance are... odd and unnatural."

"Are you not interested in dark stories?"

"It's not that I'm uninterested. It's just that, the way he shows interaction feels out of place. Plus 'The Raven' became a bit repetitive with its diction." For the first time, Olivia finally had the chance to critique another writer, and it felt like she had just vented out her deepest frustrations all in one sentence.

"Damn, what happened to Brennan?" a boy sarcastically said, turning to her. "Usually you act like a jackass, but today you're actually being bearable."

"Settle down," Mr. Heart told him. "And Brennan, thanks for your insight."

After that, the slideshow ended, and the class was left to stare at a blank screen. Their teacher let out a sigh and said, "I hope you guys have some inspiration now." From there, he pointed to the girl at the front of the class and told her to hand out pieces of notebook paper, but once she passed by Olivia, and they both made eye contact, the girl was quick to break it as she left her with a frown and a piece of paper.

Olivia shrugged it off and moved her pencil to the top of the page. She wrote her name, but then stopped to erase it. She vigorously scraped the eraser against the page until no pencil mark was left to be seen, and only then did she write Brennan's name. She got straight to working, and used her current scenario to write a drama and thriller story.

After only fifteen minutes of writing, Mr. Heart decided to walk around the class to check on everyone's progress.

"What do you have?" he asked one student.

"A romance story."

The closer Mr. Heart got to her desk, the more Olivia's leg would shake up and down.

"What's your story about?" he asked, standing next to Olivia.

She looked up at him and smiled. She recounted the main plot points of the story she imagined, and Mr. Heart grinned as he placed a hand on her shoulder.

"There's something different about you today," he said. "But I'd say this change is a good one."

Olivia appreciated the tiny gesture of approval, but she wondered what it was about Brennan that everyone detested. As he began to walk by another student, Olivia made it her mission to write down a few more pages for her story, but her concentration was cut short when Brennan's phone vibrated in her pants. She discreetly pulled it out and caught wind of multiple text messages as pop-up notifications. Olivia stared at the caller ID and noticed the number read *(360)904-2789.* Olivia realized she knew that number. She thought back to all of the conversations she'd overhead and how each of her peers wanted to get a hold of that number. It was someone they'd placed on a pedestal. A person that for some reason everyone was interested in. Who was it? Olivia shut her eyes to focus in on her memories.

Suddenly, Jessica's face popped into her mind. Olivia began to recall Brennan's off-the-wall personality causing a bout of uneasiness to surface. What if he worsens her relationship with Jessica even more?

While Olivia was too busy looking at her phone, she failed to notice the fact that Mr. Heart had caught wind of it. He stepped towards her and tapped on her shoulder. "Come and talk to me after class," he whispered.

"What?" Olivia said, turning her head.

"Just see me after class. You're not in trouble. I just need to talk to you."

"Oh, okay," Olivia sighed as she put the phone back into her pocket.

The last twenty minutes of class went by uneventfully for most of students, but to Olivia it was just a tornado of imagined events running through her head. She became so lost in writing her story that those last twenty minutes seemed to take up an hour. As she invested herself in her own plot, the bell rang, signaling the end of class.

The rest of the students gathered their papers and shoved them down their bags.

Olivia, however, took the time to carefully bring them together and organize them appropriately in Brennan's bag, but for her the session wasn't over yet. She dreaded having to talk to Mr. Heart, but she was never one to refuse a request by authority. She kept her head down and gradually made her way towards his desk.

"Well, hurry up," Mr. Heart said, motioning for Olivia to come closer. "Like I said, you're not in trouble. I just wanted to ask you something. I just want you to know that there's always help being offered when needed. We have counselors you can talk to and they can direct you towards other community resources." He said that as directly as he could, without leaving behind a hint of hesitation, and Olivia got the impression that he was referring to Brennan's suicide.

"Oh well, okay..." Olivia stuttered.

"Mrs. Walker seemed to have a hard time in your absence. She was crying a lot."

At this heartbreaking news, Olivia blushed, even though she knew she wasn't responsible for Brennan's actions. The despair showed on her face and her lip started quivering.

"I see," Mr. Heart said understandingly. "We had a teachers' meeting today. They told us to keep an eye on you kids. They emphasized that your well-being took precedence above all else, and I know why. You know, the funny thing about this is that we only ever talk about it when it hits us."

"Well, I don't know what to say," Olivia stated.

"Don't worry about it. I just want to make sure you won't do the same thing again, but let me ask you something before you leave."

"Sure." Olivia sounded unsure of herself, but she pressed on anyway.

"I know you can be pretty extreme sometimes, but to imagine you ending things is just too much. Could you tell me why?"

Olivia's face turned red, and she turned her head to the floor. "Even I don't know the answer to that," she said. Brennan remained an enigma to her. What could his reasons be for ending his life? All Olivia saw was a sister who loved him, and teachers who were willing to support him.

Mr. Heart let out a tiny chuckle that was audible enough for both of them to hear. "Sorry, I'm not laughing at you. It's just that... I had a friend like you back in my high school days. He said the same thing. But I guess that sometimes in the heat of the moment you tend to forget everything else. It doesn't apply to everyone, and

I'm confident it doesn't apply to you. I think you know why. It's just that you're too afraid to say it."

This struck a chord with Olivia, and although she was truly oblivious of Brennan's reasons, she completely knew what her own reasons were. There were so many times she wanted to vent out or tell her life story to someone, but the fear consumed her like a blanket, and it pulled her down into a void of loneliness. Once that realization stabbed her heart, she began to shed tears, but these tears were different. They came out as tears of relief rather than sadness. Relief that someone out there finally had some understanding of her, but the crushing weight of despair came from the fact that this man was right. She was scared and she still is.

"You don't have to cry anymore," he said sternly but comfortingly. His voice showed strength and reassurance. It was the kind of aura that her stepfather failed to radiate. "I can already tell your experience has changed you. Change can be good, but there's always a limit to change."

"Th-thank you." It took all of Olivia's strength to muster those words and she hoped that Brennan would come to his senses and learn what she'd learned.

"Go out there and *seize the day*," he said as a farewell, and with that he wrote out a pass for Olivia so she could have an excuse for being late to her next class. She walked out the door, but not before turning around to thank him again.

The walk to the next classroom was still a hectic mess among the chaos of students trying to get by, but having Brennan's schedule in hand made it survivable.

Up next was Mrs. Walker's class. It took considerably more time for Olivia to find her classroom since it was in a different building located off to the side of campus, but eventually she arrived at the right building. The hallway in this wing had cement flooring, and there was definitely a draft nearby that chilled many of the students. When she entered the building, ahead of her was a straight path that broke off into a left turn. Olivia went straight down and checked the classroom to her left, but Mrs. Walker didn't seem to be there. Instead, a male teacher with a heavy build could be seen drawing on a chalkboard. Olivia turned her head away and continued down the left corridor, while checking every classroom she came by. When she finally landed next to the graphic design room, she read the name 'Mrs. Walker'. The label was neatly printed in a frame next to the door, and the moment she took her first step into the class, Mrs. Walker's eyes greeted her with a friendly look.

Other than that, each student was sitting in front of their computer waiting for the period to start so they could either work or doze off for the next hour. An empty cubicle sat across from Mrs. Walker's desk. and Olivia assumed that that was where Brennan used sit. As she passed by her peers, most of them kept their head out of view to avoid eye contact, while a couple of them snicked as she went by. Once she got to her computer, she flopped down on the chair, making it creak.

"Good morning," Mrs. Walker announced to the class.

"Good morning, Mrs. Walker," they all said in unison.

"It's just going to be a regular day. Continue doing your work," she told them.

Olivia turned on her monitor and got ready to log on, but she was blocked by a password. *Crap.*

The details of the password must've been common knowledge to all students. Would it seem too out of the ordinary if she asked for it? Her finger began twitching over the spacebar as she let the rest of her fingers hover over multiple keys. Eventually, she gave up and shot her right hand into the air to signal for Mrs. Walker's help.

"Yes, can I help you?" Mrs. Walker asked politely.

"I forgot the password." She gave her teacher a watery smile, hoping for pity.

"It's 'green'. The best way to remember is that the username is the same as the password." Mrs. Walker pointed to the username at the top right of the screen, and sure enough, it said "green".

"Thank you," Olivia said, relieved.

The computer took a good five seconds to completely start, and when it was done, Olivia was introduced to a wallpaper of the whole class in one big picture. There were rows of students with each one of them smiling at the camera. She took another good look at the photo, hoping to catch an image of Brennan. She found him hidden in the back row without a smile to show, and among other things the desktop was cluttered with shortcuts to different files that had been left behind. Each project had a practical name rather than a creative one, such as "Teacher Poster One".

Out of curiosity, Olivia felt the sudden urge to sort through all of Brennan's artwork. She double-clicked one of the files, and the screen was filled with an image of a park bench. In front of it was a light blue background with stars dotting the sky. The next piece was simply labeled "Ink Bottle Logo". The artwork was just an image of an ink bottle drawn out with a company's name in the middle, and upon further inspection, Olivia found that he took the time to show the bottle with two different color schemes. One was black-and-white while the other was light blue and dark blue. Ultimately, after witnessing these two works, Olivia felt a little disappointed. Of course, to her, Brennan didn't seem like the artistic type, but without a doubt he was definitely a better visual artist than she'd ever be. The last file had a vaguer name, which made it stand out amongst the others. All it said was "Forlorn", and Olivia wondered what it could mean. She clicked on the file and took a minute to take in what she saw. The background was a dark green that faded into a lighter color as it went down the page, but the focus was a young girl in the middle of it. The painting was a close-up of her from the chest up. From the looks of it, she had a yellow dress, and short black hair that reached the bottom of her neck. She wore a cute little ribbon, but the biggest detail was that her head was stuck in a fishbowl. She stood up while the bowl was flipped upside down, so it fit snugly over her head like an astronaut's helmet. The glass seemed to be filled with water, and the girl kept her eyes closed and mouth formed into a frown. The liquid didn't seem to be pouring out. It just stayed in the bowl as if gravity didn't exist. Inside were goldfish swimming in front of her face, but each fish had an abnormal body. Their structure was simply made up of words that each held a strong meaning. One fish said "why" while the other said "leave". Olivia's eyes scanned each fish until she noticed a pattern. Each body had a word and she found out that when put together, they spelled out a sentence.

"Why... did... you... leave..." Olivia quietly read. She sat back in her chair, and the girl on the screen seemed to be silently crying out for someone to hold her.

Mrs. Walker's footsteps echoed behind Olivia and ended right next to her with a big smack on the ground. "What inspired you to make that?" she asked.

Olivia turned her head to face Mrs. Walker, but then turned back to the screen. "Maybe there's just something about me I don't want to admit, or maybe I'm just a little sad," Olivia muttered.

"Do you really think that?"

"I'd like to say, 'yes' as though I knew the answer, but I really don't."

Mrs. Walker's eyes narrowed on the screen as she got lost in thought. "I guess your mind is a different story from your outward appearance."

And as she said this, Olivia knew she was right. What was it about Brennan that she had yet to fully understand?

Chapter Six

The layout of Olivia's school was much larger and more convoluted than Brennan's, and with absolutely no knowledge of her schedule, Brennan found himself skipping all of his classes for the day, the only exception being Mr. Jefferson's class, which he found with Jessica's help. Brennan made sure not to lose track of her as they walked side by side through the labyrinth of hallways. He noticed her trembling more as they got closer to the classroom. It was the same kind of anxiety he saw in his sister, back when they were kids.

"Hey, Olivia," Jessica said in a soft voice.

"What?" Brennan asked plainly.

"When we get in there, everyone's going to welcome you back, even my friends, but…"

"But what? Isn't that a good thing?"

Jessica stopped right outside of the classroom and grabbed Brennan by the arm to bring him to a halt. "I know I haven't been the nicest person to you, but please don't ditch me for them. You're the only person I've talked to since you collapsed that day."

"Don't worry, I promise, but can I ask you to make one too?"

Jessica gave him an odd expression. "I'll keep my promise if you keep yours."

"What do you want me to do?"

"If I stick around you, at the very least help me get to my friend. You know, the one I mentioned earlier, Brennan."

"Yeah, I'll do that."

Jessica gave a smile and giggled. "At the very least, tell me more about him."

"We can talk about him later. I'd rather just get in class and be done with it." After that, he casually pushed past her and strode into the classroom. By the time he put one foot through the door everyone gave a big gasp. Some were staring at him with wide eyes, while others found it troubling to make even a slight amount of eye contact. Brennan noticed that Mr. Jefferson had no words to say. Even though Brennan didn't know him, he got the idea that he knew Olivia well. Maybe he knew her as well as Mrs. Walker knew Brennan, and he guessed that Mr. Jefferson must've been shocked to see Olivia back on her feet already.

"Welcome back, Olivia," Mr. Jefferson said to break the silence. "I hope you've recovered well and fully."

Everyone was nodding in agreement.

"Thanks," Brennan said cautiously.

He noticed a desk in the back by the window that had a big poster on it. There were dozens of signatures all over the paper, and at the very top in big bold letters read "Get well soon." Assuming that it was Olivia's desk, Brennan briskly made his way over there, with Jessica eagerly trailing behind him.

"Jessica!" Mr. Jefferson yelled, making her freeze.

Her eyes seemed to pop out of her face, and Brennan unexpectedly felt worried about her.

"You won't be sitting next to Olivia anymore. In fact, I don't even want to see you near her." Mr. Jefferson raised his voice and sternly folded his arms across his chest. "Well, am I being clear?" he asked.

"Yes, I understand," Jessica said.

"What did you say?"

"I said 'yes, I understand'." She raised her voice, so it was audible to everyone. A few of the students began to whisper to each other, but Brennan couldn't understand most of it. But he did know that the sight reminded him of the students at his school. All the gossip and hostility they showed stirred the anger rooting from his past experiences. Brennan gave a nasty look to the two students in front of him and they immediately stopped talking. However, this wasn't enough to stop everyone.

"Mr. Jefferson?" Brennan said, raising his hand.

The entire class ceased their gossip to stare at him. He didn't have any friends, but Brennan was sure that if he did, he wouldn't take the initiative to defend them. After all, he had a mentality of "survival of the fittest". But Jessica's company seemed to seep under his skin. Just like his sister, she was there for him, but unlike his sister, she didn't leave him. "Take it a little easy on Jessica. She's not as bad as you think she is. She –"

"Olivia, I know you're a kind person, but you have to realize that what I'm doing is for your own good."

"No, you're wrong, I –"

"Olivia, please stop. Just settle down, okay?" As Mr. Jefferson continued to ignore Brennan's arguments, he said to Jessica, "You'll be switching seats with Max here at the front of the class."

Max nodded and reached down to pick up her bag, and as she and Jessica crossed paths in the center of the room, Brennan noticed that despite the situation, Jessica still made sure to smile at her classmate as they walked by.

"Can't believe we were ever friends," Max muttered, and she gave a big smile to Brennan as she sat down next to him.

On the opposite end of things, Jessica sat down and gently laid her head on the desk. She quietly cried to herself, but the sound was still loud enough for Mr. Jefferson to hear. He took a moment to stare down at her but didn't say anything, and just went on ignoring her in favor of returning his attention to the class.

"Now I want to talk to all of you about something I find very important in creative writing." Mr. Jefferson spoke loudly addressing the entire class. "This is what I call the 'perfect victim.'"

Brennan slumped over his desk, trying to suppress the urge to march to the front of the class and smack their teacher in the face.

"Are you okay?" Max asked. Out of the corner of his eye, Brennan saw her reach out to tap his shoulder, and he quickly slapped it away. "Listen, if Jessica bothers you again, you could always hang out with me and my friends. You don't need her." Listening to her felt like having a snake whisper in his ear. To Brennan, his habit of distancing himself from others was disappearing very quickly. Jessica wasn't someone he could lose. He kept telling himself that he just wanted to use her to get to Florida, but after seeing everyone turn their backs on her, he was beginning to think of her as an outcast. Just like he was...

As Mr. Jefferson continued with the lesson, every student gave a confused look, but no one raised their hand to ask a question.

"There are times when writers will attempt to make you feel sympathy towards a certain character," he said. "I mean, I'm pretty sure we've all seen it."

A few of the students showed no interest in the lesson at all, including Brennan, but some of the more insightful ones nodded their heads.

"Tell me what makes you feel sympathy for someone." Mr. Jefferson left the class with that open-ended question. *Surely not someone like you.* Brennan gritted his teeth as he tried to zone out Mr. Jefferson's voice.

"How about them being relatable?" a student said, while raising his hand.

"Yes, that's one reason. How can we feel sympathy for someone if they're too out of touch with reality, right?" Mr. Jefferson ceased talking and the spotlight went to no one. "Come on," he said egging them on. "What makes you feel sympathy towards another human being?" After about ten seconds of silence, Mr. Jefferson randomly picked on Max to give an answer.

"I didn't raise my hand," she said nervously.

"Oh, I know, but I want you to give me an answer," he stated.

"Well, I um..." she stuttered over her words, turning it into a salad as she rubbed the back of her head. "What about... their... their flaws," she said aloud.

"You're on the right track," Mr. Jefferson happily exclaimed. "Flaws are one thing, but what about their past experiences? I'm pretty sure we all feel sorry for someone who has had a traumatic event happen to them."

As he said this, he locked eyes with Brennan and eventually everyone was fixated on him.

"I agree," Brennan said uncomfortably.

His saying that it seemed to break everyone out of their trance.

"Well, I'd like to point out that most readers only feel sympathy for a certain personality type," Mr. Jefferson said. "I call it 'the passive persona.'" He clapped his hands together and smiled at the class, and Brennan wondered where this lesson could be leading to. "Often when we see the most sympathetic characters, they're usually cowardly and passive. It pulls you in and makes you believe that they don't deserve the wrong treatment they're getting. After all, they're shown to us as being weak and unable to fend for themselves."

The class listened intently as the lesson progressed.

"But we must remember that people don't always turn out that way." Mr. Jefferson coughed to clear up his throat. "Often in the real world we see people turn out for the worst, especially if they've had an abusive past. They're still victims, so why don't we feel that much sympathy for them?"

"What makes you so sure of that?" Brennan asked out loud. All heads turned to him.

"Olivia, you're not acting like yourself today. Is everything okay?"

"Oh, I'm absolutely fine," Brennan sighed. "I'm just wondering if you have any self-awareness at all."

Mr. Jefferson shifted his body, and Brennan could feel tension building between them.

It was only dissolved when Jessica bravely raised her hand to answer his original question. "I think it's because they turned out to be just as bad as their trauma, or even worse. Unlike the passive character who is still innocent and –"

"Thank you. That's enough," Mr. Jefferson interrupted, and Jessica frowned. "It seems that we only feel sympathy for these troubled characters when they're shown to have a soft side," he continued. "I don't know about you guys, but I'm always one to feel sympathy for either character, but that's just my personal opinion."

Jessica lifted her head from her desk and glared at him, and even Brennan did the same thing. "Sure, you feel sympathy for troubled kids," she muttered sarcastically.

"What's that?" Mr. Jefferson asked, overhearing her.

"I can't stand this bullshit," Brennan muttered to himself.

Max turned to him. "I don't mean to sound rude, but...What's going on with you? Mr. Jefferson, me, my friends, and everyone else is on your side. You don't need to defend Jessica."

Brennan ignored her and turned his attention towards the front of the class.

Jessica lay back in her chair and exposed her tear-stained face. "You only showed compassion to the students you found 'easy'!" she yelled at Mr. Jefferson as loud as she could. "You know, those fuckers that do everything you say and have no depth to their personality! Or how about the fact that you never tried to understand the rest of us who misbehaved?"

Not once did Mr. Jefferson flinch. "Tell me, Jessica," he said quietly. By 'troubled students,' are you including yourself?"

At this Jessica turned her head away with a soft grunt escaping her throat, but she recomposed herself in her chair and tried to take another stance on the argument. "I – I... Yes..." she finally admitted. She closed her eyes in what seemed to be an attempt to avoid the glares her peers were giving, and much to her delight, Brennan wasn't one of them.

"Well, what is there to understand about you?" Mr. Jefferson asked Jessica. "A bully like you drove one of our students to the edge," he said, referring to Olivia. "Oh, and sorry," he added, looking at Brennan.

However, Brennan didn't dare speak a single word. Instead, he just stared at him, wondering what kind of teacher would have the audacity to say that. Brennan jumped out of his chair, catching everyone's attention. "Stop!" he yelled. By now, acting like Olivia was completely out of his plan. *Fuck blending in! And fuck this guy!* It didn't take long for him to realize, but Mr. Jefferson was everything Brennan hated in a person. The lack of self-awareness, the condescending attitude, and his constant gaslighting was too much for him to bear.

"Olivia, I know you've been experiencing some really strong emotions lately, but –"

"Shut the hell up! You can't treat her like this," Brennan said, referring to Jessica.

Mr. Jefferson averted his eyes from Brennan and looked at Jessica.

"I just want you and everyone else to know," Jessica said, "that you're a bunch of fucking hypocrites." Following in Brennan's footsteps, her body seemed to shake, and for a moment Brennan sensed that all the students were recognizing the anger Jessica would always give off, but he felt something different about her this time; he knew that this type of fury came from something bottled deep inside.

"Shut up!" Max yelled out from the back of the class. "We all know what you did!"

"Listen. Listen to me!" Jessica said in an attempt to regain their attention, but the crowd was too busy jeering at her like a mob of spectators at an execution. From all the laughing and snickering, none of Jessica's words were audible, and so she gave a big sigh, stood up from her chair, and with all her strength she bent over to grab the legs of her desk. She hoisted it over her head, but before the situation reached its conclusion, a few students took notice of her actions and stopped. They tried their best to point her out, but everyone was too busy laughing at her expense. It was only when Jessica wailed and slammed the desk on the floor that everyone completely fell silent. A leg broke off the table and toppled on the ground, making it the only sound that filled the room.

"Wow, way to go, Jessica!" Max said sarcastically.

"Shut the fuck up and listen to me, you delusional bitch!" Jessica yelled and pointed a finger at her former friend. "The same goes for everyone here! Don't single me out. I know I bullied Olivia to death, but can't you understand that I'm trying to grow as a person? And don't act so innocent. We all know for a fact that I wasn't the only one who bullied her. You all laughed along with me as I said the most terrible things straight to her face!

"And you!" she said, poking a finger at Mr. Jefferson. "You didn't do shit! Don't act like you're the hero for turning the tables on me."

From there, Jessica turned around and faced the entire class. "Be honest. You guys would still be bullying her if she didn't try to kill herself, and now that she actually tried it, no one wants to accept their part of the blame. We're all responsible for her attempt."

By the end of her speech, Jessica was winded and was breaking into a sweat. She turned to glance at Brennan and he nodded.

"I – I..." Jessica broke apart hysterically and ran out of the classroom in a frenzy. She charged through the door and slammed it shut on the way out.

"Wow, what a bitch!" Max said aloud, and the entire class laughed. She turned to Brennan. "Don't worry, Jessica won't bother you anymore."

By the end of the whole ordeal, Brennan had formulated a higher opinion of Jessica. No doubt she had pointed out a clear flaw, and he could see himself in her shoes, because, just like in his previous life as Brennan Claufield, everyone had turned their backs on him and isolated him from the herd. Jessica may have been a bully, but she was a damn relatable one. By now, just her relatability was enough to make Brennan want to stick around.

He stood up, which caught the attention of everyone in the room. They watched him quietly as he headed towards the door.

But before he could leave, Mr. Jefferson turned to say, "You can tell me what's wrong."

"She's right about you guys," Brennan said before abandoning the classroom.

Brennan's feet raced like his heartbeat as he ran down the hallway, hoping to be right on Jessica's tail. In front of him was a long stretch of floor with lockers lined up against the wall, and even though this made it difficult to see around corners, out of his peripheral vision he noticed the fleeting image of a girl taking a right turn. Her footsteps stomped loudly, and Brennan followed the sound as closely as he could. When he reached the corner, the girl seemed to have vanished.

The entire hallway was empty except for the janitor, who was just waddling his way out of the boys' restroom. He sluggishly lugged his cleaning equipment in front of him without taking notice of Brennan.

"Hey! Hey!" Brennan yelled at him as he stepped forward.

The man turned around and raised an eyebrow, and with his short stature he forced Brennan to look down to him.

"Did you happen to see a girl run down here?" Brennan asked, breathing heavy.

"Why do you need to know?" The janitor asked. For a moment he kept a serious face, but that soon faded away and turned into a chuckle. "You kids better not be skipping class, but if you're looking for your friend, I think she just went into the restroom."

Brennan nodded his head and mistakenly ran to the boys' restroom.

"Hey, where do you think you're going?" the man yelled. This time his joking demeanor and friendly presence had disappeared.

"Oh, I'm sorry. I guess I was just on auto pilot." Brennan slowly let go of the door handle, and with his palms trembling, he walked to the girl's bathroom with his head down.

"Fucking kids," the janitor rudely muttered, but Brennan ignored his comment and pushed through the bathroom door.

"Jessica?" he called once he entered the room. Brennan stayed silent waiting to hear a reply, but there was none. Rather than discouraging him, he felt a strange feeling sweep its way in. It was the same sort of thing that entered his head when he was at the train station. Sweat dripped from his head, and his ears began to tune into every little frequency that could be heard. His breathing became much more apparent, and in his own mind he felt like an animal trapped in a corner. Somehow, he knew he wasn't alone in there.

"Jessica?" he said, this time more softly. He quietly tiptoed his way to the middle of the bathroom while still trying to pick up anything out of the ordinary.

"Hmph."

Brennan's ears twitched at the sound of whimpering. It didn't sound like the kind one would hear from an animal. Instead, it was the kind of sound one would hear from a girl trying to suppress her screams. Brennan's left ear picked up on the silent scream coming from one of the stalls.

"Jessica, it's me, Olivia. You can come out now." He tried his best to make a soothing tone of voice, and, much to his amusement, he did quite well, which must've been due to his new feminine vocal chords. He turned to face the stalls and stopped for another couple of seconds. He held his arms out, hoping that Jessica would barge through one of the stalls and fall into them.

"Jessica?" he said again, audibly. In return, he heard a louder suppressed cry coming from the last stall closest to the wall. He briskly paced over there, and gently extended his arm out to gradually open the door. Once he pushed it about halfway, it came to a stop when it made contact with a person's body on the inside. "Jessica, I know it's you."

After hearing that, the girl moved to the back of the stall to get out of the way of the door, and sure enough Brennan found Jessica snuggled up in the corner, with tears streaming out of her eyes. She took one look at Brennan before screaming out loud.

"Don't look at me!" she yelled. With her foot, she tried to kick the door shut, but Brennan shoved his shoulder forward to prevent that from happening.

"Relax," he grunted. By now, he was fighting against the force of her legs, and after a moment or two of struggling, Jessica stopped resisting until she came to a complete stop. "Just let me talk to you," Brennan sighed.

However, she didn't say anything. Instead, she just put her head down and cried harder, like a little girl.

Brennan squeezed his way inside and closed the door behind them. He slid his back down the wall and sat down in the corner next to Jessica. He leaned his head back and stretched out his legs. "I just wanted to talk about what you did in class earlier," he said.

"I don't want to talk about it."

"I was just going so say that I thought it was badass. You know what I mean?" Brennan leaned forward and playfully punched her arm, and when she turned her head to look at him, he gave a genuine smile. "You've got some balls," he laughed out.

Jessica stopped crying and sniffled. "You really think so?" she asked. When the tears stopped streaming out, Brennan could tell she was starting to feel better.

"Yeah..." Brennan said dreamily. "Reminds me of this one time when I told one of my teachers to fuck off."

"Did you really?"

"Yeah. What? You think I can't stand up for myself?"

"I just can't see you doing something like that. Are you really Olivia?"

Brennan's body jerked forward, and he let out an uncomfortable laugh while wondering what Olivia would've thought about this. "People change," he said softly.

"Well, they do, but do they change that quickly and drastically, or have I just never seen you for who you really are?"

"Maybe a bit of both." Brennan smirked and stretched his arms over his head. In his mind, he wanted to do this best to impress Jessica, but he began to notice that he was doing nothing more than confusing her. "I'd like to say that I've changed, but maybe I haven't." Since seeing Life and Death playing together, he'd had some time to reflect. Haniel's words still echoed in his brain:

You're like a whole different person now. Not only that, but meeting Jessica and seeing how happy she made him had started to make Brennan want to change his negative outlook on life. "I think you've changed too."

"Hey, what's that supposed to mean?" Jessica eyed him curiously and pursed her lips out as though she suspected that Brennan wasn't being entirely truthful.

"Why does it seem like you don't believe me?"

"Well, I've just never seen you like this." Jessica nervously crossed her arms over her chest. She twitched her toes back and forth as she sat there with her head against the wall.

"I like the person that you are," Brennan told her.

"Do you really?"

"Sure, I do." Brennan turned his gaze towards her, and for a while they sat staring at each other without saying a word. Brennan felt the tension growing between them until he decided to break it with a smile. He grinned at her, and in return, a smile eased itself upon her lips. "Come on, let's get out of here." Brennan stood up and offered Jessica his hand.

"No, thanks," she told him. "I think I'll just stay here until I hear the bell ring."

Brennan looked down at her with happiness showing on his face. He was already feeling the euphoria of talking to someone so like-minded.

"Oh, alright. I guess I'll see you later."

"Yes, I'll meet you in the cafeteria," Jessica said, still quiet.

Brennan strode out of the bathroom feeling a sense of accomplishment.

By the time he reached the classroom, the bell had already rung, but considering that he'd left his belongings behind, he deemed it necessary to return. As soon as he reached the door handle, Max pushed it open, accidentally slamming his nose. "Shit!" he yelped. He held his nose and grunted in pain.

For a moment, Max didn't realize what had happened, but when Brennan yelled, she immediately apologized.

"Oh, I'm so sorry!" She went in to hug his pain away, but Brennan held his arm out in front of him.

"Don't worry, it's fine." He shook his head and rested his arms by his side.

"Hey, why don't you sit with us at lunch?" Max said. "That way you don't have to worry about Jessica getting to you." She smiled as if she were performing an act of kindness, but Brennan knew that it couldn't be further from the truth.

He'd already set his mind on being by Jessica's side, and he didn't plan on breaking that promise. "I'll think about it," he lied as he went into the classroom.

No one followed him in, so for the moment he was alone with Mr. Jefferson, who sat at his desk by the whiteboard, but Brennan didn't care to catch his attention. He hurried over to his seat by the window and picked up the few pencils he had left behind and shoved them in his pocket.

"Where's your bag?" Mr. Jefferson asked. "I usually see you lugging that heavy thing around."

"I just didn't bring it with me today." In the back of his mind, Brennan wanted to get out of there as quickly as he could. Sparking up a conversation with Mr. Jefferson was the least of his concerns, but much to his dismay, Mr. Jefferson wanted to have a little chat with him.

"Before you go, I need to talk to you," he said.

Brennan turned his face away, shut his eyes, and bit down on his lip.

"You know, if Jessica or anyone picks on you again you could always –"

"Yeah, yeah, I get it," Brennan quickly interrupted as he went on to dismiss himself from the conversation.

"Wait! I'm not done here!" Mr. Jefferson called back. "Just know that I'm serious about what I said. If Jessica picks on you again –"

"I said, *I get it!*" Brennan raised his voice, which caught them both off guard. He hadn't planned on defending Jessica again, yet here he was. "She's not a bad person, I assure you."

"Look, you've always been gentle, and it's admirable, but you need to realize that some people are out there just to hurt you."

"Oh? And what about everyone else?" Brennan asked with aggression. "Didn't they bully me into oblivion too?"

"I'll admit, I did see some of that, but they've since apologized for what they did. And I think we all knew who the ringleader was."

"Are you *blind*?" Brennan yelled. There were so many times in his life when he had been singled out, and here he saw the same thing happening to Jessica. Even though he didn't care about that many people, witnessing harassment of the few he'd made a connection with, made his face turn red. "She's changed. I know she has." Brennan may not have experienced firsthand how Jessica treated Olivia, but he managed to catch bits and pieces of it through the words and actions of his classmates.

Brennan was sure that their descriptions had failed to fit Jessica's personality now, and as always, Brennan was sure of his conviction. Right now, the only person on his mind was Jessica, and he had to get to her.

"Do you honestly believe that people change that quickly?" Mr. Jefferson asked.

"I'd like to believe that. Maybe Jessica's making that belief come true. Either way, I'm done talking." Brennan walked away and took one last glance behind his back.

"Olivia..." Mr. Jefferson said.

However, Brennan ignored his pleas and headed out the door.

His eyes drifted down the hallway. He noticed everything in his surroundings. From the group of girls chatting around their locker to the mundane act of a student sipping from the water fountain. Being back in such a familiar yet new place had a surreal feeling to it. Walking through the hallways while watching everyone else took him back to that day – the day he walked out of school to hang himself. But there was something different this time. Someone was waiting for him, and that someone was Jessica.

Brennan barely remembered the quickest path to the cafeteria, so he guessed that he must've left Jessica waiting longer than he should have, but once he finally entered the spacious lunchroom, he scanned the area for her. First, his eyes darted towards the center of the room where the circular tables lay, but she wasn't there, and neither was she in the line of students waiting for food. Brennan thought it'd be best to wander around the center of the room to be able to see most of his surroundings. There seemed to be some railing around the center that enclosed the space in a square shape. He ran his fingers through the rails as he walked beside it.

Where is she?

She wasn't sitting by the giant windows that looked into the cafeteria, nor was she milling about at the far end by the double doors, but once Brennan went by his entire side of the railing, his foot bumped into a set of stairs. Up on the second floor seemed to be where most of the older students were sitting. He strode up the steps and was greeted by the sight of a few more tables that harbored the upperclassman of the school.

"She'd better be here," he told himself, and luckily for him, she was.

At the top floor where he stood was a catwalk that hovered above the ground floor and led to the rest of the classrooms on the second floor, but most of the catwalk was guarded by a locked gate. Jessica rested her head against the gate, looking down at the students below.

"Jessica!" Brennan called out to her.

But the rowdiness of the other students swallowed up his voice, making it inaudible. He picked up the pace and ran towards her. Brennan gently tapped on her shoulder with his finger, and Jessica's eyes dashed to him almost fearfully. She had a horrified expression as though she wasn't expecting Brennan's sudden arrival.

"Don't be so jumpy. It's just me," he laughed.

Jessica smiled brightly at him, but then came a curious look. "Where's your lunch?" she asked.

"Oh, I didn't pack one, and I don't have the money to buy food."

Jessica turned her head away in shame. "Sorry, I didn't take the time to pack you something last night."

"Hey, don't worry about it. You're not my mo—" He stopped mid-sentence, and Jessica seemed to catch wind of this.

"What were you going to say?" she asked.

Despite her question, Brennan was confident that they both knew what word it was. In his vocabulary "mom" was a forbidden word, but of course, Jessica didn't know that.

"I'm fine without eating." Brennan did his best to brighten her day, but she still seemed sullen from earlier. "So, I'm guessing this is where you usually eat?"

Jessica shook her head shyly causing Brennan's mind to wonder.

"No? Where, then?" he asked.

Jessica pulled him closer to her and put her lips to his ear. "I'll share my lunch with you if you promise not to tell anyone." She giggled in a quiet tone, and Brennan pulled his body back to smile nervously at her.

"Not tell anyone about what?" he asked.

"I'll just show you my favorite spot to eat. Watch our backs."

"Right now? Where are we going?"

"Just trust me. You'll love it." Jessica's hand motioned for Brennan to turn around and he did. What he was looking for, he didn't know, but he made sure to keep an eye out for both staff and students. Luckily for both of them, no one even took the time to glance in their direction. While Brennan acted as their protector, Jessica turned to face the gate. It stretched out to touch the wall, but on the left side was nothing but air, since it marked the edge of the catwalk. Jessica hastily reached her arm over the railing and behind the gate. It was locked from the back, but she managed to stretch her arm far enough to reach the lock. She quickly fidgeted with it until it gave way.

"Olivia, over here," she whispered.

Brennan turned around to find her opening the gate slightly. It was just wide enough for them to barely squeeze their bodies through without gaining any attention. Once Jessica had slipped through, it was Brennan's turn, and it came to him much easier. His frame managed to fly through the open crack like it was non-existent.

"Where are we going?" he asked.

Jessica glared at him and put a finger to her lips. "I'll tell you once we get to the other side."

She grabbed his hand and quickly led them across the catwalk until they were safe from everyone's view, and once they disappeared, Brennan took a moment to lean against the wall to catch his breath.

"Already winded, huh? You need some exercise," Jessica lectured.

"Don't worry," Brennan said in between gasps of air. "Usually I'm not like this."

And while he tried to recover his strength, Jessica headed towards a set of only four steps that led to a metal door.

"Where's that lead to?" Brennan asked her.

"The lock doesn't work. I always go through here." She pushed open the door and a ray of sunshine assaulted her eyes. For a moment she shielded herself before going through, and then Brennan followed her. Once they exited the building, the wind blew on their faces, and Brennan felt the cold air of Washington again.

"Why are we on the roof?" he asked.

"Ever since people have been treating me differently, I like to come up here. Get away from it all, you know?" Jessica took off her jacket, feeling indifferent to the chill in the air, and set it down to use as a picnic blanket. She sat down and patted the empty spot next to her. "Come on, sit with me."

Brennan dropped on his bottom and sat crisscrossed.

"How are you not freezing?" he asked, shivering.

"I'm just used to it." Jessica pulled out her lunch box and tore her sandwich in half. She gave one half to Brennan, and he ended up taking a bite that made most of the sandwich vanish.

"Hey, Olivia."

"What?" Brennan asked through a mouthful of food.

"Do you hate me?"

"I might've been acting like a dick lately, but no."

"Thanks." Jessica gave him a sideways hug which almost made him choke on his lunch. He went into a violent coughing fit, forcing Jessica to toss him her water bottle.

He quickly gulped it down, sending the food into the depths of his stomach.

"Olivia, how come you're always so nice? It's like you never hate anyone, not even me."

Jessica's comment made Brennan wonder what kind of person Olivia really was. The differences in their personality were like night and day. Olivia's kindness shone bright like the sun, and Brennan's heart was cold like the night.

"Am I really that kind?" he asked, hoping to get an insight into Olivia's life.

"Okay, well... Not recently, but before then. You never showed hatred towards anyone. Even when they deserved it."

"I guess I just don't really know myself at all." Brennan was mostly referring to his lack of knowledge about Olivia, but for a moment he thought of himself. With so many mixed feelings about the day, and his newfound fondness for Jessica, his world view seemed to be turning upside down.

Jessica lay down on her back and clasped her hands behind her head to use as a makeshift pillow.

"In any case, good job on calling out the bullshit in Mr. Jefferson's lesson," Brennan said, and he turned his head to look at her, but she frowned.

"He's a hypocrite. He acts so self-righteous when he's in the wrong." Jessica rolled over on her side and gritted her teeth over one of her fingernails. "All he cares about is looking good to the rest of the world. That guy always –"

"Hold on a minute," Brennan said, interrupting her. "I remember you pointed out that he doesn't care for 'troubled kids'. From what I get you were talking about all the misfits, kinda like..." Brennan wanted to end his statement with "you", but that just didn't seem right. He considered all the friends she had, and realized that at some point she wasn't a misfit. She was wanted.

"Kinda like what?" Jessica asked, irritated.

"Like *you*... Or at least, *the new you*."

"So, what about it?"

"Do you really think anyone actually cares for people like you? Well, not just you, but pretty much every other misfit and outcast out there?" Brennan hated people who put down others, and he especially hated those who did it while in a position of power. To him, misfits needed just as much love as everybody else. Brennan's eyes covertly gazed at her and Jessica's expression looked downcast.

"What are you saying?" she asked.

"Would you really care for people like that? You know, those bastards that make a mess of everything, and always seem to be causing trouble? Because I can tell you, people don't care about kids like us."

Jessica sat up straight. "I wouldn't consider you to be a misfit," she said, confused.

"Don't... don't think about that for now," Brennan stuttered. "Remember how you said I didn't seem to be that 'nice person' I was before?"

Jessica nodded her head.

"Well, imagine if I was always like that. If you knew all the things I dealt with. Would you still care about me?" Jessica didn't say anything, and so Brennan brought it upon himself to continue. "Just think about this. According to Mr. Jefferson's lesson, even these 'troubled characters' have dealt with a traumatic past, which is what causes them to act out in unconventional ways. Now think about yourself. Why can't people see that those who get hurt, hurt others?"

She brought her knees close in to her face and sank her head in between them. "Let's not talk about that for now," she said.

Brennan placed a hand on her shoulder to comfort her. "Don't worry. Whatever it is you've been through, you're the way you are because of it. But remember, it's still up to you how you turn out." Brennan scooted closer to her and embraced her in a hug.

It seemed that through all of this, he'd had a revelation of his own. "I want you to listen, and listen carefully," he said. "I know how it feels. Everyone like us is shut out and we're treated like trash. The ones we care about leave us behind, and –"

"Olivia, why do you talk about yourself like you're a completely different person? I mean, this doesn't sound like you at all."

"Shh, just listen to me," he shushed her. "You've made me realize that I may have been a cunt because I let my past experiences define me."

"What happened to you?" Jessica seemed to be growing concerned.

"Did I ever tell you how much I hated my mom?"

"I thought you *loved* your mom. You'd always talk about how much she cared for you, and she even made your stepdad tolerable."

Brennan stumbled over his words, but he quickly shook his head and put any idea of Olivia's life away. "Whatever I told you before, just forget it," he said defiantly.

"But why?"

"Just shut up and listen to me. I don't want to explain why."

Jessica's facial expression changed, and Brennan could tell that she was confused at the sudden change of events.

"I've come to learn that, in life, people will always fail you. It's true. It's happened to me and my sister. And guess what? My sister left me too. Everyone is going to fail you. I might even do the same if I haven't already. It seems that we're inherently bad and we'd do our best not to show it to the world. Instead, we hide it deep down and behind closed doors. No one knew my mom would beat the shit out of me and my sister. And just like you, everyone turned their backs in favor of looking good."

"What are you getting at?" Jessica asked, leaning into him. "And since when did you have a sister?"

Brennan paused for a moment, but realized he couldn't come up with an elaborate story about a long-lost sibling. "Sometimes... I just speak... on autopilot." He felt stupid for saying it, but for now that excuse would have to be enough. "I just want to tell you how the world works. I'd say people like you and I are completely justified for being jerks, but the rest of the world sees us as nothing more than a bunch of brats. They completely forget all the bullshit we experience, and only focus on our bad behavior. That's why they don't feel anything for us, and they'll hate us even more if we're a spitting image of them." Brennan fell on his back and looked up to the sky. He watched the clouds, and inhaled the cold air, reminiscing of the trips to the park he'd take with Nora, but the thought of opening up to Jessica even more scared him.

Brennan rolled over on his side and tugged at her sleeve, prompting her to turn her attention to him. "Stay here with me. Forget the lunch bell. I'm not going back there."

Without saying a word, Jessica followed his instructions, and she laid on her side facing him.

"Can you promise me something?" he asked. Brennan's hands were sweating, but he couldn't help it. This was the first time he'd opened up to someone that wasn't his sister. But most importantly, it was the first time he'd ask someone to be his friend.

"What?"

"Despite the way I've been treating you for the past few days, can we still be friends, and I mean good friends?"

Jessica gave a soft smile and a tear escaped from her eye. "Only if you promise to do something for me."

"And what would that be?"

Jessica gave a short chuckle in response to his words. "Tell me more about yourself. Tell me everything, and leave nothing out. I just want to learn more about you."

"Why?" Brennan asked, bewildered.

"Well, it seems like I obviously don't know anything about you at all. Everything you said came as a complete surprise to me, and I want to hear more of it."

"I can do that, but I also have a favor to ask of you."

"Oh?"

"When the time comes, go with me to Florida. I think my friend, Brennan, would get along quite nicely with you. He could use a friend like you."

Jessica's smile returned once he said this. "Is he anything like you?" she asked.

"I... Well... I don't know how to answer that." Brennan rolled over on his back and proceeded to lose himself with his train of thought as he wondered if he should explain his situation. "I just think the three of us could have some fun together. You, me, and Brennan."

"So, you're not going to answer my question?" Jessica pressed on.

"Like I said, I don't know how to answer that." Brennan knew he was revealing too much about himself without considering what Olivia was like, but he just couldn't help it. He needed someone to talk to... someone to connect to... and so he avoided Jessica's question to buy himself some time.

"Oh, alright," she said. "I trust you."

"You know what else you should trust me with?" Brennan smiled at her and giggled.

"And what would that be?"

"How about the idea that staying up here for the rest of the day would be more fun than going back to class?" Brennan smiled at her and waited for an answer.

At first Jessica seemed hesitant, but eventually she caved in. "Fine, if you say so, but don't blame me if we get caught."

"Don't worry about that. I have a plan for everything." Brennan rested his head into his hands as he lay on his back, smiling at the sky. Maybe Jessica wasn't as bad as everyone thought. Brennan's stomach felt like his organs were churning, but in a way that was different from before. While Jessica may have caused him a bit of stress, it was a good kind of the stress. It was the kind of stress that made him want to talk to her over and over again, and in a way, he kind of missed that stress. Seeing as how his time with her wouldn't last forever, the idea of their parting lingered, so Brennan decided to treasure the moment. And even though the urge to create distance still presented itself, he just held on to a mental image of his sister. Jessica could be the support his sister wasn't.

After lying there for a while, his mind began to go blank and the organs in his body stopped churning.

For the first time since the hospital, he felt a true form of bliss.

Chapter Seven

Olivia decided to spend her lunch break sitting in Mrs. Walker's class. She sat in front of the computer, searching through Brennan's work history. Even though she didn't really have any skills in visual arts, looking at artistic work calmed her down, and with the unnerving feeling that she needed to find Brennan, that need for calmness came in droves. The last time she spoke to Brennan he seemed hot-headed as usual, which made her worry about him acting out on his own. Why was he with Jessica, her sworn enemy? Olivia couldn't stop thinking about him spending time with Jessica, and so her leg began to shake.

"Hey, Brennan?" Mrs. Walker said.

Olivia turned her head to look across her desk where she sat. "Yes?" she replied.

"Why are you always shaking? Is there something bothering you?"

"Do I really shake that much?" The accusation had piqued her curiosity since she never saw Brennan as the type to get anxious.

"Yes, actually quite often. You're also very jumpy." Mrs. Walker stirred the food in her lunch box while waiting for Olivia to say something.

"I guess I just haven't noticed it before." Olivia rubbed her chin and turned her attention back to her screen. She skimmed through folders of Brennan's artwork which were scattered about with no organization at all. Her eyes narrowed in on the labels of each folder, hoping to find something that would hint towards their current class project, but she didn't find anything. Even if there was a hint, it was probably lost in a sea of images Brennan had created. Olivia grunted and rolled her eyes.

Why did he stop keeping track of everything? She let out a groan. Just the thought of being disorganized made her stomach want to hurl.

"What are you looking for?" Mrs. Walker asked.

Olivia jumped and nervously locked eyes with her. She had to think of an excuse quickly.

"See, you *are* jumpy," Mrs. Walker commented, and chuckled.

"How did you know I was looking for something?"

"Don't you know? I get the privilege of being able to monitor every computer screen!"

"Huh..." Olivia assumed that Mrs. Walker must've talked about this bit of security at the beginning of the year. "Oh sorry. I said I was going to work, but I guess I just got distracted."

"It's fine. Just tell me what you need to find, so I can get to it." She smiled at Olivia, eager to help.

"I forgot what our current project in class is."

"Okay." Mrs. Walker let her word roll off her tongue and linger in the air for a moment. "Did you really forget?" Her cheeks blushed and she scratched the back of her head. "I guess I just gave you guys a boring project to work on..."

"Oh no, it's not that!" Olivia jumped and raised her hands to say sorry. She never meant to offend Mrs. Walker, but at that moment she seemed unsure about herself. "My memory is just bad." She shrugged her shoulders and gave an awkward smile to use as damage control.

"Surely you can't forget that quickly," Mrs. Walker questioned, leaving Olivia to think of an excuse.

"My memory has just been hazy these last few days since I... Well, you know..."

"Oh, I see... Well, if you have to know, we're making posters for the literature club here at school."

'There's a literature club?" Olivia asked excitedly. For a moment, she became excited and wanted to join, but her main goal of meeting Brennan resurfaced. *No time for relaxation...*

"Yes, they've had fliers plastered against every wall in the building. I guess you really were gone for that long..."

They both stared at each other without saying a word, and the only hint of communication they had were their concerned faces.

"Anyway, that's about it," Mrs. Walker said.

"Okay," Olivia muttered. "So, when do we start this project?"

Mrs. Walker gave another sad look and stared up to the ceiling in wonder. "About three weeks ago," she said, without gazing down.

"Oh, I see." Olivia considered her answer and proceeded to search through Brennan's artwork. She sorted each project by date and took into account the time frame Brennan would've started the project. Maybe he already started it before his death, and she'd have something to work off. She scrolled her mouse wheel down the page, but there was no recent file that clearly labeled itself. Most pieces of his work were organized with names relating to their project, but as she kept scrolling, she noticed more ambiguous names.

"He's got some good stuff in here," she whispered to herself. "The layout is just confusing."

"What was that?" Mrs. Walker asked, having overheard her speak.

"It's nothing. I'm just looking for the work I already did for the project." Olivia exhaled a puff of air and moaned in frustration.

"Well from what I see, you've become very disorganized. Maybe you should take your time to sort out your work."

At the top of the computer was an icon that said, "Sort by date", and Olivia moved her mouse cursor to the top and clicked it again. Then each file became organized, from the most recent to the oldest. From there it became very clear that the closer the date was to his death, the more disorganized his work became. Olivia's couldn't help but ask herself why. She noticed a piece titled "Scattered words" and she double-clicked it open. In less than a mere second the screen was filled with an image of a black pencil writing on a piece of paper. It was from a sideways point of view and the writing utensil seemed to break apart at the end into a cluster of random letters that floated towards the top of the screen. Each object was shown to be black, but not made of solid color. Instead, they were shaded as though it wasn't made on a computer but rather a drawing on a piece of paper.

Looks complete to me, Olivia thought to herself, and she hoped that she wouldn't be forced to improve upon something in which she had no skill.

"Did you find it?" Mrs. Walker chimed in.

"Yeah, I did, but I think I'll just go to the bathroom for a moment." She got up from her chair and went to the bathroom to splash her face with water, but before leaving she looked up at the clock above the doorway. The time was almost twelve o'clock, so pretty soon the hallways would be flooded with students again.

On her way out, she hugged the side of the wall and kept her hands in her pockets. It wasn't something she'd usually do. However, she kept some of her old habits by walking with her head down. Although it didn't come without its consequences. While facing the floor, she was completely blinded to anything in front of her, so she only noticed a pair of feet just a moment before bumping into someone. Their heads collided in the air and they glared at each other.

"Brennan," the girl said sadly.

"Who are you?" Olivia asked, confused.

"Don't pre-pretend," she stuttered, tapping her two index fingers together as she made her best efforts to avoid eye contact.

"I'm sorry, but I have to go." Olivia made it her goal to get out of the way of another awkward moment, but the girl seized her sleeve. "What?"

"I... I..."

"Just tell me what you need to say," Olivia said in a hurry before taking a moment to reflect. "Sorry, I guess I was being a bit rude. Take your time."

"I know why you were gone for so long," the girl whispered.

"I figured news like that would spread fast." Even though Olivia didn't completely know or understand Brennan's life, she figured that something like this would be noteworthy.

"Mrs. Walker cried a lot, and I did too. Actually not a lot – just... just a little..." This was new to Olivia. Did Brennan have any friends? Hopefully, that meant she'd have someone to work with. Maybe someone who could give her a free ride to Washington.

Olivia looked deep into the girl's eyes without saying anything, and the hallway went silent for the next few seconds.

"Don't worry about me. I'm better now," Olivia said. From then she was just about to walk away and to the restroom, but Olivia caught another whisper escaping her lips.

"Is it my fault?" the girl asked.

Olivia stopped dead in her tracks and turned her head to look behind her. She wanted to find out more, but she knew she had to choose her words carefully.

"Why don't you tell me why you feel that way?" Olivia gave a fake smile which must've been unlike anything Brennan would've done, but she was trying her best. The need not to offend others even at her own expense was strong. But when she noticed the girl hesitate, she decided it might be best to save the conversation for later. "Why don't we talk about it later?" she said with a tiny smile, and as she headed towards the bathroom.

"I'll see you in Mrs. Walker's class," the girl said.

Olivia ran the water in the sink and plunged her face into it. The cool liquid felt like a baptism, washing away all the frustration. After her short journey into the sink, Olivia looked at her soaked face in the mirror. Ever since waking up in the hospital, she did her best to prevent herself from doing that. Seeing Brennan's face instead of her own still felt surreal, almost as though she were watching his life through a camera lens.

"Who is this girl?" Olivia said to her reflection. Maybe she could give insight into Brennan's life, but what if she brought Olivia more trouble? That girl did seem pretty horrified. *Did Brennan do something to her?* She sniffled and wrung the water out of her hands. She paced the bathroom while conjuring thoughts and scenarios of what could've happened. *Did Brennan hurt her? Was he close to her? Shit – what am I going to do?* Olivia's teeth started chattering from the anticipation, and she bit down hard on a fingernail, making a piece of it pop off. Eventually she wiped away the water with her shirt and inhaled deeply. *Just talk,* she told herself. *Just talk things out and it should go smoothly. What's the worst that could happen?*

She strode out of the bathroom with a phony display of confidence. She swung her arms by her side as she acted out what she saw those confident men in movies do.

Mrs. Walker's class would be her home for the next hour since lunch ended, and once the bell rang, Olivia already heard the stampede of footsteps closing in on her. There must have been about thirty students getting ready to run into the same room as she was, so she made haste towards the door and quickly got in before being engulfed by the entire student body. When she got inside the room, she peered down to her desk and noticed that the girl was sitting in the same cubicle as her. She used her chair to spin in circles to pass the time. By now, Olivia anticipated their chat that would soon happen, and so she tried to bide her time. First off, she gradually walked to her own desk without lifting her head to avoid anyone starting at her, and when she reached her chair, she slammed her butt down.

"Hey, Brennan," Mrs. Walker said, "since you were gone, I'll give you extra time to complete our project." She turned her seat to face her with wide eyes. Mrs. Walker's happy expression was in marked contrast to Olivia's grief-stricken face. "Brennan, you could help Elly with her side of the project. What do you think?" She pointed at the girl Olivia met in the hallway.

"I'm fine with that," Elly said while staring at Olivia.

"Sure," she said shyly.

After that, Elly turned to face her monitor and logged onto the computer. Olivia stood behind her and looked past her shoulder. She felt envious at how all of Elly's files and artwork were neatly organized with a name that distinctly showed which piece was for which project. Elly simply titled their current project "literature club poster", and when she clicked the file for one of the programs on the computer, it showed every content that was added to the piece.

Her artwork depicted an ink bottle that toppled over, letting it cover a big portion of the screen with a dark blue. However, the ink didn't just turn into random splotches. It split apart into three different streams that came together in the center to spell out "Literature".

"What do you need help with?" Olivia asked.

"It's nothing. Just tell me what you think."

"It's creative," she commented. Critiquing art wasn't something she knew how to do effectively, but she thought that if someone could judge her writing without being a writer, then surely she could evaluate a piece of art without being an artist. Elly continued to make edits, and the sheer amount of tools within the program confused yet amazed Olivia at the same time.

"Why did you do it?" Elly asked, getting straight to the point.

It took a moment, but Olivia finally realized what she was asking.

"Oh, I..." There were no words that she could come up with. "I really don't know," she said nervously.

"Do you not know, or do you just not want to tell me?"

Elly's question put more pressure on Olivia, but she didn't cave in. Instead, she folded her arms and reminded herself to act abrasive just like Brennan, but she just couldn't, so she took a moment to decide how she could answer her question without being rude.

"I'll just tell you when I feel more comfortable. Just give me some time." Olivia made sure not to sound like a confused child. And much to her relief, it worked.

Elly began to relax her shoulders as she accepted her answer, but from then on, the clock would be ticking. Olivia knew that without a doubt Elly would come back seeking an answer, and she would have to deliver it. What shook her body was that Brennan was the type of person to hold in his pain. His suicide letter to Mrs. Walker was obvious proof, and so she knew that there must be a lot to Brennan's life that she didn't know. Olivia pressed her hands against the sides of her head and ran her fingers through her hair. Stress was starting to build up again and she had to fight off the temptation to shrink into her body.

After Olivia took the time to calm down, she turned her chair around to face the monitor. From there she put up a front that she was working. She opened up the typical programs she guessed Brennan would've used, and randomly clicked on different tools. Other than that, Olivia still carried Brennan's phone in her pocket, and it had become a useless piece of hardware at this point. As she contemplated how to bring the phone's usefulness back to life, she'd steal glances at the clock from time to time.

What could the passcode be? Unlocking the phone might give her a means of contacting Brennan regularly, and the thought of the amount of information on the device would be imperative to knowing him. Olivia turned on the phone and stared at the empty passcode space. What could it have been? A birthday? Part of an address, or something stupid like 1, 2, 3, 4? The last option was a long shot, but Olivia decided it was worth a try, and much to her expectations, it didn't work. "Damn," she muttered. She sat there and wondered what Brennan would do if he were there. For sure he was the type of guy who kept his secrets, but Olivia still fantasized the relief of not being kept in the dark anymore – although she remembered that their relationship didn't even evolve into a friendship, and as far as she was concerned, it was pretty one-sided. After the phone screen turned red to indicate that it locked itself, Olivia couldn't do anything but be frustrated for the next five minutes. "Locked out again," she muttered.

"What's wrong?" Elly asked as she rolled her chair closer.

"I forgot my password."

"I can help with that." Elly happily grinned and held her hand out open to show that she was ready to take the phone.

"How will you do that?" Olivia pulled her hands close and clutched the phone tightly to her chest. "What are you going to do with it?"

"Nothing bad. I do this all the time with my phone." Once more Elly held her hand out, but Olivia still declined the offer.

"I'm not handing it over until you tell me exactly what you plan to do." Olivia made her voice stern, and for once she spoke similarly to Brennan.

"I was suggesting that we just restart your phone," Elly whispered.

"But wouldn't that get rid of everything on here?"

"Yes, but it's a sure way of unlocking it." Elly nimbly tapped her index fingers together and silently sat in front of Olivia, but when Olivia didn't smile, she spoke again. "There's something else I could do," she said softly with a trembling voice. "My dad works with computers and other bits of technology. Maybe he'd be able to use what he has to bypass the password."

Olivia stared at her in amazement. This idea was definitely a breakthrough in solving one of her biggest problems, and if it worked, she could snoop through Brennan's stuff.

"Will your dad do that for me?" Olivia asked.

Elly frowned and her eyes twitched nervously. "Most likely not, but it's worth a try, and even if he says 'no' he's still taught me a thing or two. I may be able to do it myself."

"I guess I don't have any other choice. Just don't break it." Olivia handed Elly the phone and she fumbled with it as she shoved the device down her pocket.

"Don't worry. I won't let you down." She smiled at Olivia, eager to please her.

Olivia eased her guard and gave back a smile of her own in hopes that Elly would make a good friend in all of this.

Chapter Eight

By now it had been hours since Olivia's first day of school ended, and she was glad to be back in Nora's apartment. Growing up as an only child heightened her interest in her since she never had an older sister. The feeling was somewhat new and exciting for her. Who knew that she could feel so loved by someone else who wasn't a parental figure? In her pajamas, she sat on the couch beside her beloved new sister as they viewed a movie on the television. Nora rested her head on Olivia's shoulder, and her warm presence engulfed her like a heated blanket.

"What movie is this?" Olivia asked with interest.

Nora chuckled as she put some popcorn in her mouth.

"You don't remember? We used to watch this tons of times when we were kids."

"Sorry, I guess my memory really is bad," Olivia said, playing along.

Nora reached over to her left side and picked up the remote. She aimed it straight at the screen and pressed the button to turn up the volume. Her body became extremely animated as the movie reached its climax.

"Remember this part?" she whispered excitedly. "Back then we'd always play that game." Nora pointed to the siblings on the screen playing hide-and-seek. The boy was hiding behind a door while his sister, blindfolded, was forced to track him down. Her little feet padded against the wooden floorboards and her brother held in his breath hoping, she wouldn't hear him.

"That's crazy," Olivia muttered. "How did we ever find each other like that?"

"Remember?" Nora playfully teased. "Whenever one of us says 'Clap!', the other person would have to clap their hands and the seeker would follow the noise. Of course, we could only do that three times. At least that was the rule, anyway."

"Oh, I see. That makes sense." Olivia turned her attention back to the film and Nora did the same.

"You always cheated though," Nora said, poking Olivia on the side.

"Did I?"

"Yeah, you always wore the thinnest blindfold, so you could see through it. I remember I'd start pouting, and Mom would..." Nora's voice trailed off. Her head drifted up to the ceiling, causing Olivia to be concerned.

"Would what?" Olivia asked.

"She'd just get mad at the noise. You know... All that childish screaming and running just pissed her off."

By now, Olivia's ears were wide open. At first, she wanted to learn more about Brennan's life through Nora, but now she just wanted to know more about her new "sister".

"I'm sorry," Nora said. "I just bring this up at the most random times."

"No, it's fine. Keep talking."

Nora leaned her head back into the couch and sighed. "It's just that... Mom's anger would always get the best of her. Remember when she first hit you?"

Olivia shook her head, hoping that Nora would elaborate.

"Well, I do," she said. "Mom took Dad's old belt and wrapped it around her hand so that the buckle was on her fist. Then she punched you right in the eye. It was the first time she hit you, and the first time she drew blood. You were curled up in a ball after that. The rest of that day was just a blur to me, but I do remember hiding in my room." By now Nora had sullen eyes. Her hand was shaking on top of her thigh and she kept her head down. "I'm sorry, Brennan."

"Sorry for what?" Olivia asked. Despite feeling concerned for Nora's well-being, Olivia was feeling uncomfortable. Even though she harbored extreme amounts of empathy, sometimes that empathy just became too heavy of a burden to bear.

"I'm sorry, I left you."

Olivia raised an eyebrow at her.

"The moment I was able to move out, I did. I took my chance and left. I left you behind. Even when we were kids, I would still run away into my bedroom. I rarely stuck around for you. I just ran away. I was so scared."

Olivia's throat urged her to speak out words of comfort, but she didn't have anything to say. Instead, she just stayed silent. She expected Nora to cry, but upon making eye contact with her, she saw that she was stone-faced. No tears, just a blank stare as though she were reliving the events in her head.

"There's no need for regrets now," Olivia told her. "You're with me. Let's just get back to the movie."

Nora eased her body posture, and Olivia could feel the tension starting to die, and when she turned her eyes to the television, she saw the little girl in the movie reach around the door and catch hold of her brother's shirt. She jumped up and opened her eyes, yelling, "I found you! I found you!" And after witnessing that, there was an almost euphoric feeling as though seeing such a lovely sight couldn't be real.

"I wish we could go back to that," Nora commented with a glazed look in her eyes. "Not the part where Mom would beat us. I mean the carefree part, where we could play." This time her stare turned into a bright one. Like she was in a dream.

"Hey, Nora. Do you love me the way I am?"

The daydream-like state she was in came to an abrupt end.

"Yes, of course, I do. We've had some arguments before, but this is the closest we've ever been."

"It's funny that you say that..." Olivia muttered. She thought about her own place in the world, and how she would inevitably switch places with Brennan again. But what would happen then? Would Brennan return to his old ways and suddenly Nora's relationship with him would be changed?

"What do you mean?" Nora asked with a bit of curiosity.

"Oh, it's nothing," Olivia lied. She recounted all the events that led up to the present and how differently she felt. All of the love shown to her by Mrs. Walker and Nora had made her come to the conclusion that she'd been delusional for the past few years. For so long, she'd believed that no one could help her, but she finally realized that she was just looking in all the wrong places. Maybe she would've felt the same kind of support had she only been looking properly. Olivia turned to Nora with a big smile on her face. "I just want you to promise me that we'll always be siblings."

"No need to be dramatic, we already ended that bit when I got done talking about mom... but of course. Siblings... Always..." Nora laughed and rubbed the top of Olivia's head. Her fingers frazzled her hair, making Olivia look like a complete mess.

However, when it came to the idea of Brennan returning, she couldn't help but feel a small knot being tied in her stomach, and for once the thought of going back swelled up deep inside her. Like a bottle getting ready to burst.

"Will you keep that promise? Siblings? Always?"

"You're really something, you know that?" Nora ran her hand around Olivia's back and hugged her tightly. "You don't have to worry about anything anymore. We're still siblings, and we'll always be siblings."

By the time Olivia retreated from Nora's hug she was left feeling mentally drained and Nora could see the fatigued look in her face. She turned off the television as soon as the credits started to roll, and then headed towards her bedroom.

"I'll fetch you a blanket," Nora said before leaving the room.

Olivia wiped her tears away and put her feet up on the couch. She laid on her back and tightly clutched her hands to her chest.

She closed her eyes and swallowed hard. About a day ago she asked Brennan not to interfere with her life, but here she was being a hypocrite by acting out in her own way. She held her breath for a moment and slowly exhaled. Her eyes remained shut as she tried to calm her thoughts. For the first time, her mind went blank. There was absolutely nothing in there. No happy or sad thoughts, just a blank canvas, and pretty soon sleep consumed her.

Back in the real world, Brennan was relaxing in Jessica's bedroom, and although he had promised Olivia's mother he'd return that day, the thought of Mr. Benning would intrude in his head. That man had instilled a certain kind of fear in him that no one else had. Whenever Brennan thought of him, the image of a kind old man with a sinister grin would accompany it, and while they sat on Jessica's bed, he felt like he was already living in a nightmare.

"When do you want me to drive you home?" Jessica asked.

"You're not going to do that. In fact, never bring that up again. There's no way I'm going there. Not a chance." There was a bit of a growl to his voice and Jessica looked like she was taken aback by the sudden change in tone.

"Alright then, but how are you going to convince your mom to let you stay another night? I mean that seems imposs–"

"Just give me your phone and I'll do the rest."

"Sure, but why don't you let me help you. You've helped me a lot. I think–"

"No, just don't get in my way. I can do this."

Even though Brennan could tell that he was being too abrasive again, he decided that it was just a means to an end, and a necessary one at that. As soon as Jessica relinquished her phone, Brennan dialed Mrs. Benning's phone number. A soft ring could be heard repeating itself, but no one answered. He tried again but received the same response.

"Hey, mom," he said into the voicemail. "I'm staying at Jessica's house again. I'd talk to you over the phone but obviously you're too busy to talk to me. I'll be home tomorrow, bye."

And with that Brennan hung up the phone and handed it to Jessica.

"You know she'll be wondering why you're not home yet. She'll be worried about you too."

"I know, but... Well, we can think about that later. Let's just go to sleep. I feel like turning in early tonight."

Jessica nodded and stood up. As she walked over to the closet, she took off her clothes, stripping down into her underwear.

"What are you doing?" Brennan asked, blushing.

"I'm just changing into my pajamas. I can lend you some if you'd like. I've got plenty." At first, the situation made him confused, but then he remembered that he'd do the same thing in the boys' locker room. Changing clothes in front of someone of the same gender was fine, so long as the underwear never came off. Jessica went on about it casually while Brennan was silently panicking. "Well, do you want some?" she said, turning to him, but as soon as she turned around Brennan turned his head. "There's no need to be shy. I'm fine with lending my clothes."

"It's not that! Just put some clothes on." Brennan continued to blush and made sure not to face her, but Jessica just laughed it off.

"You're acting like you've never been in the locker room before, or are you just self-conscious?"

"Neither I'm just going to go to bed."

Brennan rolled over and closed his eyes. Despite his heart racing he managed to calm down by taking in deep breaths and pretty soon he was fast asleep.

In the blissfulness of sleep, Brennan found himself in the white void with Haniel. This time, Brennan woke up sitting on a wooden chair with dozens of clocks floating around him. They kept ticking relentlessly. *Where am I?*

"Let's just call this place the 'void'," Haniel said from behind him. Brennan turned around surprised. It felt as though Haniel had the power to read minds, but considering his status as an angel, Brennan didn't think it was too farfetched.

"Why am I here again?" Brennan asked. A small portion of the ground in front of him turned, into a puddle of white murky water. From there, a chair emerged from its watery depths and Haniel walked around to take a seat.

"We need to talk," he said. Brennan took his eyes off the puddle and raised them to meet his.

"And what will our talk be about this time?"

"Do you see those clocks floating around you?"

"Yeah, of course. I can hear them too. They're pretty damn loud."

"Well, considering that clocks are meant to represent time, I think you're worried about something related to time."

"Well, no shit. I'm trying to get to Olivia as fast as I can."

"That might not be the problem," Haniel said.

"Is it supposed to be some subconscious bullshit? Can you read my inner most thoughts?"

"No, I'm just an angel, but I've been wandering around the afterlife for a while, and I know that everything has a meaning to it. Clocks always represent time." Brennan took note of Haniel's outward appearance, and for the first time, he didn't act like a giddy child. He donned a serious face while sitting with good posture.

"I don't understand what you're saying. In fact, I can't understand anything you say."

"That's why I wanted to speak with you, so we can figure out what your mind is trying to say. I've been worried about you lately.

Sometimes when I watch over you, it feels like I'm watching a caterpillar change into a butterfly."

"You don't know anything about me," Brennan muttered. "Just leave me alone, so I can finish my plan to find Olivia. I'm pretty confident that I could get Jessica to help me."

"Oh yes, that girl," Haniel said. "Maybe she's the reason you have these clocks hanging above your head."

"What does she have to do with this?"

"Well... Have you thought about what will happen once you reunite with Olivia? Will you two magically switch bodies? And even if you do... What happens to Jessica? Will you just part ways?" Brennan repeated the question in his head. Haniel brought up a good point. Since Brennan was growing fonder of Jessica each minute, the thought of leaving her left a hole in his heart.

"So what if you're right? What do I do then? Just walk out on her like how my sister walked out on me?" Brennan's tone slowly became more aggressive with each word.

"I can't say for sure, but at least you know your time with her is limited. You'll have to part ways at some point." Haniel gradually turned his face into a smile, and Brennan scoffed at him.

"I liked it more when you were serious." He turned his head to the side, and Haniel leaned forward.

"I'll send life to talk to you. She'll fill you in on some more details."

"Wait a minute," Brennan stammered. He focused his gaze on Haniel again. "Why do you have to be so elusive? We're sitting in front of each other right now. Why can't we just talk here?"

"An angel is always busy. I have to send someone else another message."

"Who? Olivia?"

"No. Remember when I said you two aren't the only ones in history to be brought back? I have another 'client' waiting for me. I'll see you soon." After that, Brennan's experience ended and his mind was allowed to rest.

Before opening his eyes, Brennan's sleep was interrupted by the presence of a heavy weight on his chest. There was a crushing sensation almost as though his ribs were slowly being crushed under the sheer force of something so small yet so heavy, and when Brennan finally opened his eyes, he realized what was going on.

"Life?" he said as he saw the little girl bouncing on top of him. She smiled and gave a curious nod.

"You don't look like yourself, but I still know it's you," she said in an adorable voice.

"Yeah, it's me. What are you doing here?"

Life hopped off Brennan's chest and made a perfect landing on the ground. There was an audible thud as Brennan put a finger to his lips.

"She's sleeping," he said, pointing towards Jessica. Life slowly opened the bedroom door and scurried down the steps with Brennan following behind her. "Why don't you ever talk when I need you to?" Brennan pouted like a child, but Life paid no attention to him.

"You want to see Olivia?" Brennan thought back to his conversation with Haniel. Was seeing Olivia what he really wanted to do? If he did, he'd inevitably go back to his old life. A life without Jessica.

"Of course, I do. That's why I'm going to run away to meet her," he said with false confidence.

"But Haniel said you have to do something else."

"And what would that be?" Brennan asked.

"He said, you need to go back to the train station, so you can get on the right track." Brennan rubbed the back of his head as he thought to himself. How was he going to get there? And wouldn't that be worse? Surely there wouldn't be a way to get Jessica there without killing her. In fact, how were he and Olivia supposed to get there without dying a second time?

"But how are we going to get there without dying first?"

"You could ask Haniel," Life said.

"Fine. Just tell me where to find him." Each suggestion Life had made was plundered by Brennan which didn't help. "I think I'll just meet up with Olivia and we'll see what happens next." Brennan patted the top of her head and told her that it was time for him to leave and headed back to bed. He turned around, ready to go as he mounted the steps, but Life tugged at his sleeve.

"I think Olivia is worried about you," she told him. Brennan turned his head towards her and raised his eyebrow in concern.

"Is she really?"

"Yes," Life muttered. "I think she's just worried about you and your sister." Brennan thought about it for a moment and considered the type of person Olivia was, but he gritted his teeth at the idea of Olivia tainting Nora's image of him. "Well, we'll just forget about that for now. Finding each other is more important." Brennan took one step up the stairs, but Life tugged even harder at his sleeve. "Let me go," he grunted.

"Nora says she loves you." But Brennan ignored her comment and gripped Life's wrist to take her hand off him.

"She probably just feels guilty," Brennan said. "If she really loved me, she wouldn't have left me behind." Brennan kept things vague, and Life looked at him inquisitively. This time he made haste up the staircase, but the little girl wasn't giving up just yet. She followed him to the top and once more pulled at his shirt sleeve. "What!" Brennan yelled. A sound could be heard coming from Jessica's room, but both of them were too caught up with each other to notice. Life stepped back and cowered away from him. She put her arms up to shield her face, and for a moment, Brennan felt ashamed of himself. "I'm sorry," he whispered. "I just- I just got carried away." Life put her arms down and stared at him.

"Do you want to talk to her?" she asked him.

"Talk to who? Olivia?" Life shook her head to say "no".

"I mean Nora. Your sister..." Brennan's eyes grew wide and he knelt down to put his hands on her shoulders.

"How will you–" But before he could finish, Life yelped in surprise before vanishing. Brennan turned his head and saw Jessica standing over him.

"Who are you talking to?" she asked rubbing her eyes.

"It's nothing. I was just muttering to myself. I tend to do that when I'm having a hard time thinking." Brennan stood up and got ready to head back to the bedroom.

"Well, if I'd thought you were insane, I wouldn't have let you stay here." Jessica joked and chuckled, but Brennan was in no mood to mess around. He quietly brushed past her and went to back to bed. When they were both in the room, Jessica crawled over him to get to her side of the mattress. "We have to get up early for school tomorrow," she yawned. Brennan ignored her in favor of repeating Life's words in his head.

The night went relatively calm for Olivia, except for the loud footsteps that would thud throughout the hallway, but at three in the morning they went haywire, and Olivia could've sworn she heard them coming closer. At first, they were heavy and sounded like they belonged to a giant. However, they soon became quick and light as though a child were running around. She felt the strong urge to jump off the couch to check who was disturbing her, but fear gripped her heart. Who could be out there? As always, the worst scenarios would creep into her head from a seemingly mundane event. The darkness combined with the footsteps conjured images of quiet nights with her stepfather. She pulled her blanket over most of her face and only left room for her eyes to peek out. Her heavy breath was caught under her blanket which gave a moist feeling all over her face. The footsteps echoed closer to the front door, and Olivia quickly covered her entire face. She closed her eyes and pretended to sleep, but the presence of another being entered the room and stopped beside the couch. It imposed itself onto her and she covered her mouth with her hand to suppress her whimpering. She wanted to scream but it felt like the air was being sucked from her lungs as a heavyweight plopped itself on her chest. Suddenly, the blanket was ripped off her body, leaving it exposed and forcing her to cover her face with her arms.

"Are you scared," A little boy asked. Olivia opened her eyes and saw a young boy with frazzled hair resting upon her chest, but something was off. He seemed new yet familiar at the same time, and Olivia blinked her eyes a few times to make sure she wasn't seeing things.

"Who are you?" Olivia asked as she pushed her body up.

"Don't you remember? We met at the hospital. It's me, "Death." The boy's voice was almost completely silent with a hint of sadness. "She's with Brennan," he said distantly.

"Oh, it's you!" she realized. "But who's she?"

"My sister, Life. Haniel told her that you and Brennan have to return to the train station."

"What? How?" Olivia gave a puzzled look on her face with her full attention set on the boy.

"Haniel can switch you back. You'll be yourselves again."

"Is that true?" Olivia jumped up and squeezed Death in a tight hug. He tumbled backward but Olivia was there to hold him in place.

"But I'm not sure. Life doesn't always tell the truth. Sometimes she doesn't understand Haniel. She doesn't understand a lot of things," he said.

"What? Why would your sister lie about that?"

"I don't know." Death shook his head disappointedly, and Olivia thought about what his words could mean. If Life really was a tangible person she could talk to, then why would she be so cruel? After all, shouldn't someone named Life give hope?

"I'll keep that in mind," Olivia finally said. She sighed and folded her arms across her stomach, but her thoughts were suddenly interrupted by the frowning expression on Death's face.

"You don't believe me, do you," he whimpered.

"I didn't say that. I'm just considering what you said." Olivia thought that Brennan might've been one to jump to conclusions but unlike him, she meticulously planned each move. Death groaned and fell backwards on the couch.

"Everyone believes my sister more than me. They always do what she says, but never listen to me. It's all because she's so happy," he pouted.

"No, don't think that way. You're just as important as your sister." Olivia gently cradled him and ran her fingers through his hair.

"Is that true?" Death looked up at her and she nodded.

"If happiness is the only emotion a person acknowledges then that's their problem, not yours."

"Are you saying that I'm always sad?"

"No, not at all. You can happy too. You're just happy in ways others don't expect."

"But my sister told me that being sad is wrong. That I should be happier." Olivia looked down at him and smiled comfortingly.

"Let me tell you something," she whispered in his ear. "If all you feel is happiness then you're not really living. I'll see if I can talk to Brennan about this in the morning." She gave a genuine smile and laid back. "Was there anything else you needed to tell me?" Death shook his head and jumped off the couch.

"Goodnight," he said.

"Goodnight."

A few hours later, Olivia woke up by herself on the couch. She patted the cushions and lifted the blanket as if it were possible for a child to hide under there. Then she yawned while stretching out her arms and legs by extending them. She turned her head to look out the window and into the orange sky. The color of the sun peeking behind the clouds just barely illuminated the room, but that was enough to provide a certain aesthetic that promoted serenity. As the clouds parted to make room for the sun, Olivia threw her legs over the sofa and thought to herself for a moment. She brought herself back to the previous night. Even though the future was filled with a million uncertainties, her conversation with Death must've been the most unpredictable factor. If Brennan was told that they could "connect", what would he be thinking about right now? The idea of making a leap of faith made her shudder and Olivia immediately ended that train of thought almost as soon as it began. The doorknob to Nora's bedroom twisted until it opened the doorway to reveal her standing there. By now she had changed out of her pajamas and gave Olivia a smile that filled her with warmth.

"Are you ready for school, Brennan?"

"Yes." Olivia hopped off the couch and straightened her clothes with her hands. Since she didn't change her clothes before passing out on the couch, they became wrinkled and uneven. Her hands went down her pant leg and around her shirt until it was somewhat straight, and after that was done, she followed Nora out the door and into the parking lot. When they got there the sun was still hidden behind the clouds and Olivia's took in the moment to feel the sensation of the light on her skin. She wondered how it could be so early in the morning and be so warm at the same time.

"Come on. Get in the car." Nora sat in the driver's seat and waited for Olivia to step inside, and once she did, Nora started the vehicle and pulled out of the lot. As they drove by the different neighborhoods and buildings, the scenery made Olivia feel like she was living in some sort of fever dream. A dream where she would contact Brennan. Possible as soon as Elly gives her his phone back. She rolled down the window and laid back with her eyes closed, and for some reason, she felt that this would be one hell of a day.

On the other side of the country, Brennan was just waking from his deep sleep. He sat up using his arms and looked around the room. By now, the lava lamp had burnt out and Jessica's side of the bed was empty. All that was left was an imprint of her body. Brennan figured that she must've woken up ages before he did, and so he jumped out of bed to groggily walk down the stairs. He heard the clanking of dishes as well as the refrigerator opening, and when he took a peek around the corner, he saw Jessica pouring herself some cereal. She took a white bowl and shook out the chunks of food from the box. After that she gently poured milk in without noticing him, but before walking into the kitchen, Brennan hit his pinky toe on the corner of the wall, and the sound of his grunting alerted Jessica. She quickly twisted the cap back on the jug and averted her attention towards him.

"So, you're finally awake," she said.

Rather than answering Brennan just rubbed his right eye and yawned. His eyes drifted all around the room until they rested on Jessica's face. He stared for a long moment. How could he leave her? His conversation with Haniel had made him realize just how dependent he was on her, and how much he was afraid to lose her. "What do you want for breakfast?" she asked.

"Nothing. I just wanted to know if you were still here." Brennan shook his head and walked back upstairs with Jessica calling out to him.

"Wait a minute." Brennan kept staring at her as he didn't know what to say. "Are you feeling, okay? You seem a little off today." Jessica cocked her head to the side, waiting for Brennan to answer.

"Yeah," he lied. "I just woke up wondering about how I could get to Florida to meet my friend."

"Why do I get the idea that you want me to take you there?"

"Because I do." Jessica turned her head away with a disappointed look.

"I know I said I'd be happy to take a trip with you, but I always said that the distance changes things. I can't go that far with you. Maybe in the summer, we can take a trip."

"I can't wait that long," Brennan said, gritting his teeth. He was feeling conflicted. On one hand, going away as soon as possible was what he needed, but at the same time, that meant that he would have to leave Jessica behind by the end of it. Olivia would return to her body and he would return to his. But afterward... Jessica would just go home. Maybe she won't even be friends with Olivia. She didn't come to know Jessica as he did. "Just forget it for now. Let's go to school."

Chapter Nine

With Olivia's time zone being a few hours ahead, her day at school already started. This time the maze of hallways didn't seem so much like a maze anymore. Rather, it was more of a straight path that guided Olivia towards her next destination, but something was off this time. Through the crowd of students came a select few who would stare or at the very least take piercing glances at her. Every time their eyes met hers, they'd turn away as though nothing happened. Considering how each odd interaction made Olivia feel uneasy, she decided to head outside into the courtyard where she saw a familiar face sitting on a bench in a grove of trees. Despite the surface being made of stone, she seemed to be comfortable while fidgeting with a few small tools. Olivia brushed pass the other students, the basketball court, and everything else just to get to her, and by the time she did, a strong feeling of relief came.

"Hi," she said. Elly took her eyes off her tools and looked up at her. "What are you doing?"

"This." Elly smirked and lifted Brennan's phone and small tools to Olivia's face. She showed her the insides of the device. It seems that she used the miniature tools to pry open the back and reveal the insides. Olivia took a moment to take in the information.

"Did you break it?" she asked. Fear washed over her face, and she stared at Elly as though she were accusing her of a serious crime.

"No, not at all. I just opened it, so I could mess the hardware. Pretty soon I'll be able to unlock it for you."

"But you do know what you're doing, right?"

Elly nodded her head and smiled at her. "My dad may have told me 'no' but I still remember what he taught me. I should have it done by tomorrow." Olivia nodded and sat down on the bench next to her.

"Thanks," she said. Elly turned her head to face her, and for a moment she stopped, and Olivia could feel the tension rising between them. She didn't know what it was, but for some reason, she got the impression that Elly felt very conflicted. Her face seemed distorted just like her feelings.

"How are you doing," Olivia said, trying to make small talk.

"I'm fine. It's just that I don't know what to do next. I mean when I figured out what you did to yourself, I felt a little lost. I know you never noticed me before but... I just feel a little lost without you." She leaned back and smiled. Even though the conversation had turned into one of grief, there was a bittersweet taste to it, and Olivia was still glad to see Elly's demeanor change. Unlike yesterday, her face lit up and that nervousness was completely gone. The only problem that lingered was just a small bit of awkwardness. "Listen, Brennan, can I ask you something?"

Olivia cocked her head and stared at her, wondering what could be going through her head. "Sure, what is it?"

"Are you doing anything this weekend? I mean... we could go somewhere. Anywhere. We could even fix your phone if you'd like. As long as it's something we can do together, I'm fine with it." Each sentence that came out her mouth went by faster and faster until eventually her words were so fast, they became incoherent. And at this point Olivia was starting to put the pieces together. She figured that Elly was a nervous girl who tried to stick around her as best she could, and so the thought that she might have a crush on Brennan crossed her mind. Seeing as how the day had already taken an unexpected turn, Olivia got up from the bench, trying to back away.

"I'll think about it," she said. Elly frowned and turned her head away.

"If you don't want to hang out with me that's fine," she muttered.

"No, it's not that. I just have a lot on my mind, but I think I can make some time for you." Olivia let out a nervous laugh before leaving for Mr. Heart's class, and as she walked away, she couldn't help but feel guilty. Elly was just such a nice person, and she had a useful skill, but taking advantage of someone wasn't anything Olivia would ever consider. Her eyes may have been looking forward but in the background, she believed that Elly must've been left feeling disappointed.

"Wait," Elly yelled at her as they caught up in the hallway. "How about we just fix your phone right now?"

"But we have class starting soon. We shouldn't–"

"Never mind that," Elly interrupted. "You always skip your classes anyway." She stopped and stared at Olivia, making her feel uncomfortable.

"I know, but it just wouldn't feel right this time." Olivia turned away and began walking, but Elly placed a hand on her shoulder.

"I know this phone is important to you. You just have to skip one class and then I'll be out of your way. I promise." Elly gave her wide begging eyes until Olivia caved in.

"Fine, just tell me where to go," Olivia said.

"Well, the old woodshop class should have a bench and some extra tools. Plus, the teacher doesn't teach during first period so it should be empty for now." And before Olivia could respond, Elly grabbed her hand and led her all the way to the classroom. She ran them down the hallway and out the door into the adjacent building. Compared to the other wings, this one had a stone floor that made the atmosphere even colder. "It's this way."

Elly led Olivia to a wooden door with a window in the middle of it. The name tag next to the door had been scrawled out, so only the letter "E" in the teacher's name was visible. "Most of the time they forget to lock the door. Hopefully, we'll be lucky."

When Elly twisted the knob the door gave way and a smile appeared on her face. She immediately pushed it open, and Olivia stepped through. The smell of fresh wood and oil littered the place, but Elly didn't seem to mind. Instead, she made haste towards the first bench and laid out her tiny tools while searching for more gadgets.

As she worked on the phone she tried to make small talk with Olivia. "So, how was your morning," she said awkwardly.

"It's alright, I guess. At least I got to see the sunrise." Elly nodded as though it were relatable before quickly jumping back into the conversation.

"Were you able to see the sunrise when you were at the hospital? I mean, I'm sure you had a rec room with windows, right?"

"Yeah," Olivia lied. "I did, and it wasn't that bad over there." The memories came flooding back to her. From the suicide attempt to the stay at the hospital, everything suddenly came back. She felt like her mind was being poisoned with bad thoughts and pretty soon, she slumped her shoulders.

"You don't seem too happy about that," Elly commented.

"You're right I don't. Why don't we just leave it at that." For a moment they went quiet, but Elly just didn't seem to be able to keep her mouth shut.

"Can I tell you something?"

"What?" Olivia asked, irritated.

"My big brother was like you. By that I mean, he was also sui–"

"I get it," Olivia interrupted. She felt bad for interrupting her, but she wanted to put the discussion of suicide away. Not only that, but Olivia didn't feel comfortable thinking about someone killing themselves and not coming back. Failing to be resurrected was probably a common thing in the afterlife, but she just wanted to embrace the fact that she and Brennan were an exception.

"Anyway, before he killed himself, my dad told him 'The late teens to early twenties is a hard time in any man's life. You're always trying to find your way in a world that hasn't welcomed you, and you always feel the..." Elly stopped for a moment. Olivia looked at her and noticed that she was staring at the ceiling.

"Is everything all right," Olivia asked.

"Yeah. I'm just trying to remember what he said." She hummed until she started her speech again. "... feel the - need to prove yourself, and each time you try, you always fail. However, what's more, important is that you keep trying. You keep persevering because that type of strength is what defines, not just a man, but anyone.'"

"Your brother killed himself... I'm sorry."

"At the time I didn't know what he meant," Elly said, ignoring her previous comment. "But now that I think about it, my dad probably knew what he was talking about, and to tell you the truth, I'm afraid to graduate. My brother felt like a confused child trying to navigate the adult world. I'm afraid I'll fall apart. I'm afraid I wouldn't know what to do."

Initially, Olivia didn't notice the small droplets of tears escaping Elly's eyes but now she did.

"I'm sorry about your brother," Olivia said. "And that part about being scared to graduate, I feel that too."

"You remind me of him. You remind me of my brother."

"So, is that why you wanted to hang out with me on the weekend? Because I reminded you of your brother?" Elly silently nodded her head and continued working. "Please don't hurt yourself again, Brennan."

"I promise, I won't." And with that Olivia moved closer to Elly to comfort her. She ended up crying into her shoulder while Olivia patted her head. "I'm sorry. Really, I am." From there the two of them continued to bond.

The rest of the day went gray. From the time they left the workshop class to the time the final bell rang; it was all gray. Even in Mrs. Walker's class, there was barely any happiness, but Olivia assumed that was the price to pay for being honest and open, so by the time she left the front doors of the school, she was racking her brain to be functional.

Despite this, she knew that her next destination would be the parking lot, and on her way there she jostled against her fellow peers without even considering their personal space. Eventually, as the scene turned into a mosh pit, she felt disgusted. Not only did she get a strong stench of each boy that passed but being that close to someone always made her feel uneasy.

Her stomach would churn and wiggle when another person did so much as touch her. Only a select few people such as her mother, Nora, and now, Elly would have the privilege of coming close. Her heart began to race faster until she finally escaped the entire student body. The humidity in the air stuck by her, allowing sweat to stick to her clothes, and Olivia wondered why Brennan kept such warm attire despite the constant heat. However, once she reached the exit gate, she gripped the hot metal and pushed hard. By the time she was finally off campus, she found herself in a large parking lot that might as well have been a death sentence. Every student drove recklessly without paying much attention to their surroundings. Yet somehow, Nora always found a way to safely park, and just like all those other days, she was successful. When her vehicle came into view all that lay between Olivia and salvation was a bike rack along with some parked cars. She gave a sigh and faced Nora's car when a couple of boys from the senior class stopped by her window to have a chat.

"Hey, Nora," Olivia yelled while waving at her. The boys averted their attention from Nora.

"It's him," one of them whispered. He kept his voice low with a near-silent gritting sound escaping his teeth. "Get him," he said to his friends. Even though she was barely close enough to see Nora's face, Olivia knew that there was a hint of worry in her eyes. Olivia's heart started racing as they jogged toward her. Their arms swung by their sides and their loose shirts flowed with the wind.

"Hey," the bigger one yelled. Olivia stopped and waited for them to reach her. When they caught up to her, the guy placed one overgrown hand over her shoulder and squeezed it in a death grip. "Good to know you're finally back."

"Thanks?" Olivia said as more of a question.

"Yeah, now I can finish what we started." The boy pulled her closer, just like what her stepfather would do, and then he sank a fist into her gut. Olivia grunted and fell over.

"Wait, stop," she begged. The guy looked her up and down before kicking her in the temple. Olivia fell backward and slammed the back of her skull into the ground. Her mind became a confused mess filled with questions. She wondered who this guy was. Who his friends were, and why he would do such a thing, but it seemed like an answer wouldn't be available.

"Don't think I can just forget about what you did." He kept stomping her head into the concreate as he yelled obscenities at her. "You should've offed yourself when you had the chance." By now he was on top of her, and Olivia was barely conscious. Her eyes were fluttering shut while she tried to stay awake, but that all ended with the final glimpse of his fist connecting with her skull.

After the numbness went away, Olivia found herself in an unfamiliar place. A void of whiteness engulfed the area in front of her, but behind her stood a giant wall of photographs with each one being a picture of her. They showed her passed out in various positions. Some even looked like she was set in such a way, that she'd appear as a fashion model. Olivia averted her eyes and kept her head staring at the ground. Then much to her surprise, Haniel appeared in front of her.

"Hey!" he happily cheered. Oliva slowly lifted her head to get a good look at him.

"Where am I now," she asked. "Am I dead?" Rather than answering her question right away, Haniel pulled out a clip board with a piece of paper attached to it.

"Let's see here," he said looking down at the page. "According to these papers, you're in a coma, but don't worry about at least you're not dead!"

"Well, you seem awfully happy about that," Olivia said sarcastically.

"That's because all those events were in the past!" Haniel gave her a big smile and sat down on the ground in front of her. Even though she knew he was an angel that must've been alive for millions of years, she still couldn't shake off the impression that was still a child at heart.

"There's something I need to know," Olivia whispered.

"Oh, and what is that?"

"I just want to know what type of person Brennan was. The boy who did this to me said 'don't think I can just forget about what you did'. He wanted revenge, and I want to know why."

"Well, I'm sure you can tell that Brennan isn't the type of person who's easy to get along with."

"But I still want to know why Brennan would hurt someone so badly that they'd want to kill him."

"Do you really want to?" Haniel cautioned.

"Yes, please," Olivia begged him.

"Well then, first let me tell you about my 'angel powers.'" Haniel made ghostly sounds while twinkling his fingers in the air.

"This isn't funny. Just get to the point."

"I'll just say that instead of telling you what kind of person he is, I can show you. All I have to do is place my little finger right on your forehead and implant some of Brennan's memories into you."

"How does that work?" Olivia gave him a puzzled look.

"Oh, I'm glad you asked! Since you're in Brennan's body, it makes you two connected to each other in a way that's extremely close. Isn't that adorable?" Haniel gave a big, toothy grin, but Olivia still looked dissatisfied. "Anyway, since you're in a coma, I guess I have plenty of time to show you his life, but be warned, you'll see things you normally wouldn't want to see." Olivia slumped to the floor and laid down. She closed her eyes, waiting for Haniel to plant Brennan's memories in her head. From there she felt his finger touching her forehead. "Now, just as a warning, once we start, you'll be seeing his life as though you were actually there, and knowing him, it's going to be a little rough.

"Just do it," Olivia muttered. Without hesitation, Haniel pushed his finger inside her forehead. Olivia felt a sudden surge of energy explode in her brain as an early memory forced itself to make a grand entrance. She started writhing on the floor, and Haniel had to hold her down.

"Don't worry. It's tough at first, but I'll be there right beside you." Olivia struggled for a good minute before she was completely burnt out and lifeless.

When the memory finally surfaced Olivia's eyes were greeted to a dark room that was lit only by one candle. She heard the heavy pouring of rain outside, but most interestingly, she finally caught Haniel with a serious expression. He sat on the edge of a double bed next to an altar. The shrine was filled with pictures of Jesus along with a bible to complement it, and a few paces away from the stand was a tiny chair meant for a child. No one sat there while static on the television played out.

"Where am I?" Olivia asked.

"Just watch." Haniel pointed to the door and Olivia turned her attention towards it. A childish scream could be heard from the hallway outside.

"Please stop," a young boy yelled.

"Don't you dare run away again!" A strong feminine voice responded to his words. Olivia heard tiny and giant footsteps making their way to the bedroom, and eventually, the doorknob began to twist. The young boy immediately fell into the room and shut the door in a panic.

"Is that Brennan?" Olivia asked, turning to Haniel. He quietly nodded his head and they both braced themselves for what they were about to see.

"I already told you to stop running," the woman yelled. Olivia's ears picked up on the sound of another door being opened.

"Uh, mommy. It's fine. He didn't do anything wrong," a little girl said.

"Shut the fuck up!" A loud smack echoed through the house and the girl's voice was never heard from again. Brennan put a hand over his mouth to silence his sobbing, but it didn't do him any good. The adrenaline rush made his hands shake, and his breathing louder. Everything came to a complete stop, and Olivia started to tremble as she stared at the door. A small knock tapped on the wood.

"Brennan, I know you're in there, sweetie." Olivia knew without a doubt that this was his mother. "Please let me in. I promise I'm not mad."

"Really?" Brennan's childish stupidity revealed himself.

"Yes, now open the door."

"Can I see Nora first?" Olivia heard a loud sigh behind the door.

"You can't do that. She's in trouble too. Now, open up." She had a soothing voice. She twisted the knob and tried to push her way through, but Brennan kept his back against the door. "Let me in!" Brennan's mother began to lose herself again and she used every ounce of her strength to break through while Brennan used every ounce of his strength to resist. "Brennan, you do know that you're making your mommy angry. Now please open the–"

"No," Brennan cried out.

"You ungrateful shit!" His mother screeched and kicked the door. "When I tell you to do something, you do it! Now, let me in!" Eventually, with the sheer amount of brutality she let out, Brennan finally lost the battle. By the time he hit the carpet his mom was already in the room. Her blonde hair parted in half to reveal her stark brown eyes, and from her appearance, it seemed like she was just about to go to bed. "You spoiled brat!" She scooped Brennan in her arms and forced him onto the bed. When he noticed her heading towards the closet, he screamed. His tears started pouring out and he kicked around on the bed in a tantrum.

"No stop! Stop," he pleaded with his mom. But rather than listening, she quickly opened the sliding door and pulled out a sturdy wooden coat hanger. "No!" Brennan leaped off the mattress in an attempt to escape, but his mother grabbed him by the arm. She dragged him back to the middle of the room and shoved his head into the carpet. She raised the coat hanger high in the air before bringing it down on his face making each strike force out another tear. Olivia turned her head away to block the disturbing scene, but Haniel shook his head.

"You wanted to see what his life was like, right?" he asked. Olivia silently opened her eyes, but the sight of Brennan's mom beating him still presented itself.

"You spoiled, selfish, child! Why do I have to remember you for the rest of my life?" She screamed at his face and backed up each word with another strike. By the time Brennan curled into the fetal position, the tears were coming out relentlessly. Suddenly his mother stopped once she noticed the bruises on his face. "Why the fuck did you have to get bruised? If anyone else sees that, they'll take you away, and I'm sure you don't want to be away from your sister." Brennan's mom cooed softly while running her fingers through his hair before throwing the hanger at his eye. He wailed again, and his mother stepped out of the room while Brennan quietly cried to himself. After that, Nora waddled over to him.

"Did mommy hurt you too?" Nora asked with teary eyes. Instead of screaming, her voice became passive as he finally submitted to their mother. "Brennan..." Nora gently rubbed his hair while she sat behind him, but the comfort ended as soon as their mother came in with a bucket of ice-cold water.

"What are you doing," she yelled. Without putting down the pail, she pulled Nora by the hair and tossed her aside. The water splashed and landed on Brennan's feet, giving him a preview of what was to happen next. Nora crawled backward with the intent to huddle in a corner. She pulled her limbs into a protective shell. Meanwhile, their mom slammed the bucket down on the carpet, making more liquid spill onto Brennan's feet.

"It's cold," he sobbed.

"It's supposed to be." His mother grabbed him by the arm and pulled him up to his knees. After letting go, she tensed her hand as she grabbed his hair.

"Stop!" Brennan's little fist started slapping at her hand, hoping to loosen her grip in a futile attempt.

"We just need to get rid of those bruises!" She plunged his head into the bucket so that it was completely submerged. Air bubbles started flowing to the top while Brenna struggled. He began to throw a fit, but his mother just would just tighten her grip.

"Count to ten," she yelled, turning to Nora.

"What?"

"I said 'count to ten.' You don't want me to drown your brother, do you?"

Nora froze for a moment before snapping back to reality. She covered her ears and began counting.

"One, two, three..." Nora counted as fast as she could.

"Don't cheat. You're counting too fast." Their mom caught wind of her tactics and forced her to play by the rules.

"One." Olivia heard Brennan suck in some water. "Two." Their mother screeched again and fiercely shoved Brennan's head to the bottom of the bucket. Despite the water being there, a loud thud could still be heard. "Three." Brennan's mom raised a fist to slam on his back. "Four." Nora's voice began to break apart into violent sobs. "Five." Nora pushed her palms further against her ears to drown out the sound of her brother drowning. "Six." Brennan thrashed his body from side to side, almost making the bucket spillover. "Seven." After a few more punches to his skull, his struggling became tamer. "Eight." Brenan's mom slapped the bottom of the bucket to add more to his discomfort. "Nine." Brennan gripped the sides of the pail with the little strength he had left. "Ten! I said ten!" Nora crawled over to her mom while screaming the final number, and by the time she pulled Brennan out, he threw himself into a coughing fit while gasping for air. His chest rose up and down while he fell into his mother's lap. Rather than fighting back, he gripped her shirt while wrapping his arms around her.

"Just remember not to bother me again," she blurted out. She picked up the bucket and slammed the door on her way out. Nora went over to the bed to pull the blanket off. She huddled next to Brennan along with the sheet, and he snuggled his face into the fabric while Nora got under it as well. She embraced him in a tight hug, but rather than returning the favor, Brennan stayed still and cried.

Olivia felt shocked and guilty. She was shocked at the disturbing scene bust most importantly, she felt guilt for assuming Brennan never had any problems to deal with. "Why are you showing me this?" Olivia asked Haniel.

"I'm still digging around in Brennan's brain. I don't know what I'll bring up. These memories just come out at random". Eventually, as another memory surfaced, the bedroom faded away into obscurity. By then Olivia stood in the corner of a kitchen. The fridge and other appliances were grouped together in a section with tiled floors while the dining table stood on the wooden floor. From there, Olivia noticed a young boy who could have been fifteen, sitting across the table from a beautiful young woman.

"Nora, do you really have to move?" the boy asked.

"Brennan, you do know I'm an adult now, right? It's probably best for me to gain some independence." She smiled and put her coffee mug to her lips.

"Is that really why you want to leave?"

"Yes, I don't know what else to tell you."

"You're lying. You just want to get away from me and mom." Nora put her cup down and wiped the liquid off her lips. "Don't lie to me. You'd rather be alone than with us," Brennan said through gritted teeth.

"Hey, calm down. I'm not going to just ditch you. I'll come back to see you. I promise."

"You remind me so much of dad." Brennan folded his arms across his chest while Nora turned away.

"You have to stop bringing that up. It's been years since he left us. You have to–"

"No!" Brennan slammed his hand down. "The least you could do is stay here! Everyone leaves! Everyone! Including you!"

"I'm not like dad, I promise. Dad left after you were born and never came back. I'll come back, I promise."

"Oh sure. Next thing you know, you'll be too busy with your life, living in your own world."

"No, you're wrong." Nora leaned across the table and placed a gentle hand on his wrist. "I'll always have time for you."

"You better be right. Otherwise, you'll regret it. If no one wants me around, I'll just give them what they want."

"I promise you. I'll make time for us." Nora raised her coffee back to her lips and took a few sips before asking a question. "Why are you like this?"

"Like what?"

"I mean, why do you always feel the need to show your compassion with threats?"

"That's a stupid question," Brennan muttered.

"No, it's not. You and I both know there's something wrong with that. Why don't you try something different?" Nora placed a hand over Brennan's, but it quickly prompted him to pull back in disgust.

"I do it to keep the wrong people out."

"Is that really the truth? Cause I think you're just being stubborn because of the way Mom treated us."

"You're wrong. She's never had any control over me. Never!"

"Listen to me. If you stay this distant from everyone around you, you won't make any friends. Just some enemies..."

"Bullshit. I know for a fact that you don't hate me."

"That's only because I've known you all my life, and I love you, but no one else knows what you've been through. They don't know you like I do."

Brennan shut his eyes and turned away. "I don't need people." Brennan's lip quivered while Nora got up from her chair, and as soon as she was on her feet, she pushed the chair back into the table.

She leaned over and wrapped her arms around Brennan, but he shoved her to the floor. "Don't touch me! God, you're so stupid. First, you want to leave me and now you're trying to comfort me. You're the only one I have left, and now you're leaving. You asked why I'm the way I am, but can't you see why? Can't you see what I've become? It's all because of people like Mom, Dad, and now, *you.*"

"Brennan, I'm sorry, but I'll be come back."

"Don't lie to me." He jumped out of his chair and immediately ran up the stairs.

Nora sat on the carpet a little longer while taking the time to look up at the ceiling. It was hard to tell, but Olivia could've sworn she saw a tear leaking out from her eye.

"I think we're getting closer to another core memory," Haniel said. "Maybe this one will explain why that guy smashed your head."

"I feel sorry for him," Olivia whispered.

"Do you think what he did is acceptable?"

"No, not at all, but I can see why he is the way he is. It doesn't make it okay. It's just... sad."

Haniel hummed in agreement while his other self probed his finger deeper into her brain. Once he found the sweet spot, he applied pressure to it and the current memory faded, giving way to a new one.

This time, Olivia found herself standing in a bedroom with Brennan sitting on the edge of the mattress while burying his face in his hands.

"I'm sorry, but I just don't have the funds for it," he said to a girl sitting across the white bedsheets.

"Come on, don't give me any of that. I know you do. It's just twenty dollars. That's nothing."

"It's nothing for you, but a lot for me! Keep in mind I don't have a real job yet."

"Oh yeah, then tell me where you've been getting your money!" The girl stood up and stomped her way in front of him. She held her hands by her sides in a tight fist and towered over him, but he showed no fear, just resentment.

"In case you haven't been listening to me, I've been selling my artwork around school. It doesn't pay that much."

"I don't care. You get me what I've been asking for."

"No! Fuck, no! I'm tired of you. Every day it's the same thing. What's wrong with you? You're always saying, 'Buy me this. Buy me that!'" Brennan mocked her tone of voice which seemed to frustrate her even more.

"I won't let you speak to me that way! You're treating me like I'm a child."

"Well, then stop acting like a child. I mean you're twenty-five, and I'm just a seventeen-year-old with nothing going for him. If anything, you're the adult here, not me!"

The girl raised her hand and gave Brennan a right hook to the jaw.

He stumbled backward, but immediately stood up as his eyes flared at her. "Don't you dare hit me!" Brennan grabbed her by the neck before shoving her to the wall. Finally, her demeanor changed from one of dominance to fear. "I'm so sick of people trying to control me!"

"Get away from me!" she screeched.

"I bet nobody would even miss you anyway. Not even your brother!" Brennan raised his hand and brought it down on her left eye.

She fell on her back. Her body hit the ground like a cannon, and as her eyes grew wide, she tried to crawl backward.

"I can't stand you! I mean, look at you! You're pathetic, you know that? I mean, why would I ever be with you! All you do is whisper sweet nothings in my ear. At first, I thought you understood me. You told me that you knew what it was like to be alone, yet here you are, using me like everyone else!"

"Fuck off!" she screamed. The woman kicked Brennan in the groin to provide an opportunity to escape, and once that opportunity presented itself, she hightailed it out the door.

Olivia gave Haniel a concerned look before bringing her gaze back to Brennan. While he sat on the edge of his bed crying, Olivia began to feel conflicting emotions. On one hand, she saw Brennan as a boy who had lost his way, while on the other, he was a supervillain in the making.

"Does it bother you?" Haniel asked.

"Of course, I just don't know which part I should be bothered by. Is it Brennan, or his circumstances?"

"That's a good question," Haniel said.

"Brennan mentioned that woman's brother. Maybe that's the guy who attacked me. I just don't know what to think of him."

Chapter Ten

Brennan decided to skip most of the day by napping on the roof with Jessica, but when he awoke, for some reason he felt a stinging sensation in the back of his head. The persistence brought him down to the earth as though gravity decided to give him special attention. Dizziness washed over him, forcing Jessica to act as an escort. Even though he was barely conscious, Brennan knew that it must've been around two in the afternoon, just thirty minutes before everyone would be officially excused to leave campus.

"Jesus, what the hell happened to you?" she whispered.

"I don't know. My head just started hurting. Sorry for having you lug me around."

"Don't worry about it. You seem too messed up to survive on your own anyway." As Brennan laid his arm around her, she lifted him up an inch off the ground and carried him through the halls, and even though she had more strength than him, each step she took sucked the breath out of her.

"Don't take me to the nurse, please. They'll send me home and I'll be stuck with my parents."

"I wasn't planning to anyway," Jessica gasped. A few feet in front of them was a set of double doors. Then, without putting Brennan down, Jessica slammed her shoulder against the wood to make it give way. They both tripped, with Jessica being used as a cushion.

"Shit!" Brennan screamed. He held his head in between his hands and felt a numb tingling sensation enter his head. It felt as though someone had stuck their finger inside his brain.

"Let's go," Jessica interrupted. She quickly jumped to her feet and tried her best to pull him up. "Come on, we have to go." She heaved his weight with her shaky arms. "Up. Up. Up!"

Suddenly, Brennan heard footsteps coming around the corner. He looked at Jessica and she popped her head around the wall.

"It's Mr. Jefferson," she said.

As always, he had a neutral expression on his face and didn't seem to show much emotion, except for the occasional laugh. "I think I'm finally catching everyone's attention," he said to the other teacher by his side. Brennan could tell that his voice was coming closer, but the dizziness was too strong.

"Come on, don't give up just yet," Jessica said.

The footsteps stopped once Mr. Jefferson appeared around the corner. "Jessica, what are you doing?" he asked.

"Olivia has a headache. I was just helping her get around."

"Well, I can take things from here." Mr. Jefferson grabbed Brennan while Jessica tried to protest. His sudden movements jerked her backward and he took Brennan in his arms. "You look awful," Mr. Jefferson said.

"I just have a bad headache."

"Do you know why?"

"No, it just started..."

"Well, everything can be fixed."

By the time Mr. Jefferson stood at the front desk, the sun was glaring through the windows and assaulting Brennan's eyes.

A woman sat behind the desk, giving him a perplexed look.

"She has a headache," Mr. Jefferson said politely.

The woman nodded and led them into the infirmary. Inside were a few chairs lined up against the wall, and the far back of the room featured a doorway hidden behind a curtain. Brennan took a seat and propped his head up against the wall. The nurse hurriedly took a thermometer from her desk and stuck the tip of it under his tongue. Right before Mr. Jefferson left, they both waited for the results.

"Strange," the nurse said. She placed a hand on Brennan's forehead, but it was ice cold. "How bad is your headache?" she asked, bending over him.

"I- I..." Brennan's voice quietly died, and he began to slouch in his chair. His neck began to crane to the side as he slowly shut his eyelids.

"Hey, don't pass out on me now." The nurse snapped her fingers in front of Brennan until he opened them.

"Just lay me down, please."

The nurse stood him up and escorted him through the curtain. Brennan found himself to be in a dark room hidden from sight. He lay down on one of the beds while the nurse walked back to the phone in her office. Brennan heard the faint echo of the phone as a number was dialed. An overwhelming feeling of grief washed over him.

"Who is this?" Brennan heard a voice say.

"Hi, Mr. Benning. Your daughter, Olivia, seems to be sick. I'm afraid you'll have to pick her up."

Brennan felt the strong urge to jump up and fight for the landline, but the pain restrained him.

"I'm on my way," he heard Mr. Benning say.

From there, the nurse's footsteps boomed into the dark room, and Brennan turned to face her.

"You're making a mistake," he whispered, but the nurse didn't seem to listen.

"Your father will be coming to pick you up. Rest well."

On the other side of reality, Olivia sat in a wooden chair in the middle of a field of white.

"How long am I going to be here?" she asked Haniel.

"I'm an angel, not an oracle."

"I guess, I've never thought about that," she chuckled. She stretched her arms over her head and yawned. "Hey, can I ask you for a favor."

Haniel turned his head to her and smiled.

"If you can show me Brennan's past, could you do the same for me?"

"What are you getting at?" he asked.

"I just want to see my dad again. I don't mean my stepfather; I just want to see my dad."

For a moment Haniel's face frowned as he said, "You're still stuck in the past, huh?"

But rather than answering, Olivia slouched back in her chair and exposed her forehead to the sky. Without speaking, Haniel walked towards her and placed a finger on her skull. Olivia's chest rose as she anxiously took a breath, but it quickly fell after a few seconds. Haniel closed his eyes and probed his finger deeper into her brain. Olivia found herself to be standing in the corner of a kitchen. Rather than her dirty run-down house, the area had a certain brightness to it. On the kitchen counter sat a baby-sized Olivia looking up at her father, with drool dripping from her mouth.

He stood tall and retained her red hair. He bore jeans with a tan checkered shirt, and Olivia recognized it as a sign that he was done working for the day. It reminded her of how he would wear pajamas during his work period, since being a writer meant typing away at his computer from home.

"Let's go eat," he said, pecking her on the cheek.

The younger Olivia giggled, and she reached her arms out to touch him. He picked her up and placed her at the front of the table. She ended up sitting on a highchair with a plate of pancakes being settled in front of her. Olivia's dad handed her a fork, and while her baby doppelganger ate, the current Olivia followed her father back to the kitchen. For the first time in a span of eight years, she was finally able to walk side by side with him. She reached her arm out to hug her dad, but her limbs fell right through his torso.

It's only a memory, she told herself. The limitations hit her, and her eyes began to water. Her hands trembled as she put them over her eyelids. There was a tearing sensation in her chest as though she was a harp, and someone began cutting the strings. "I love you. I love you so much." Olivia felt a gloomy rain cloud engulf overhead when she spoke those words.

"Olivia!" her father yelled. His voice raised in pitch, and he let out a short laugh.

Olivia suddenly looked up from the puddle in her hands as she witnessed her father sitting down and having a chat with her past self. From what she saw, she remembered that her dad had no care for table manners. He continuously talked to his daughter through a mouthful of food.

"Park!" The baby Olivia chanted.

"Park..." Olivia muttered to herself. She looked across the table to her father. He folded his arms across his face with a stern look.

"No," he firmly said. Olivia noticed her younger self getting pouty while slamming her tiny fist on the wood, but that didn't break her father's attitude.

"I'm just joking. We'll go after you're done eating."

Upon hearing that, the baby Olivia shoved large portions of the pancake into her mouth.

"Slow down. We have the whole day."

At her father's soft command, she lowered her fork and ate at a steady pace. Her eyes never broke contact with the platter while each pancake began to disappear. When she was about halfway done, she leaned back in her highchair and burped. Her mouth went into an O shape. Her lips shook with the vibrations.

"I guess that's enough," her dad said.

He took Olivia out of her seat and placed her on the floor. While he went back to finish his breakfast, he instructed her to fetch her shoes.

Olivia waddled over to the front door where a pile of sneakers lay. The present Olivia watched herself disappear around a corner before turning her attention back to her father. He sat there eating, with his elbows hanging over his side of the table.

His body just seemed to take up space, and that space made Olivia feel an aura that never failed to make her smile. She took her hand from under the table and leaned her arm across it hoping to be able to hold his hand. She longed for his arms to hug her, and for him to listen to her voice, but once she came in contact in with him, her fingers slipped through. Olivia stood up from her chair and accidentally knocked it to the ground. It made a loud boom, but when she readjusted her eyes, it was magically put back to where it was.

"I wish I could talk to you," she quietly cried to him, but he didn't respond. "A lot has happened lately," she told him. "From dying, to being resurrected... a lot has happened. I've been very confused. I just wish you were here with me."

For a moment he stopped, and Olivia thought he could hear her.

In a last-ditch effort, she held her hand to his face, but when it passed through him again, she gave up. She sat back down and laid her head on the table.

"Do you still want to see more?" Haniel's voice said in her head.

"Yes." As Olivia laid her head down, she felt Haniel poking his finger around in her brain. He moved it up and down, then side to side until his intuition landed him in the center.

"Here it comes." As Haniel pushed his finger, electricity surged through Olivia's brain, and the living room in front of her turned into a quick blur as the setting vanished.

The chandelier hanging from the ceiling faded away to leave only a single light bulb. Olivia sat up and rotated her head around the room. The couches by the firepit were replaced with a twin-sized bed pushed against the wall, and the dining table was just gone. The only furniture standing in its place became a bean bag chair stationed in front of a television. She recognized the pink walls and pictures of her father. She stood behind her younger self, who was typing away at her keyboard. She chuckled after reading her screen. The only thing on it was her first short story.

She glanced at the desk to see a cupcake with a candle on it. She looked at her childish face. Her cheeks were still rounded with small bits of baby fat, and her hair was a fainter red color.

Olivia suddenly remembered what point in time she was in. Her younger doppelganger twiddled her fingers away at the keyboard while the present Olivia hopped on the bed and proceeded to lie down. She smiled at the ceiling and braced herself for the next turn of events.

After relaxing for a while, she heard a light knock at the door. She sat up and both her and her younger self stared at the doorway. Their father revealed himself to them and the younger Olivia ran up to hug him.

"Do you like the new computer?" he asked her.

"Thank you."

"I guess you do like it, huh? But I have another surprise," he chuckled and patted her head.

"What is it?" she asked.

"Well, it wouldn't be much of a surprise if I told you. You'll see it when I get back." Before he could leave the room Olivia gave him another large hug. He patted her head and left.

The eight-year-old Olivia plopped herself back in front of the desk and began typing again.

Meanwhile, the present Olivia kept wishing her father never had another surprise. As she became lost in her thoughts, she heard the sliding door of the garage lift with her father zooming out of the driveway. She put both hands on her knees and sighed.

"Olivia?" Haniel's voice said.

"Don't worry about me. I've already lived through this once."

"I can try to skip this memory. We can go to a happier time."

"No, it's fine. At least I get to see him." Olivia fell back onto the mattress and placed her palms under her head. She slowly exhaled and let the scene fade into distortion.

Suddenly she was on the couch in the living room. Her mother was crying, while a police officer spoke to her. Olivia sat on the sofa opposite her mother and watched her younger version cry out. Even without being there, Olivia swore she could hear tires screeching and glass shattering.

"Are you ready?" Haniel's voice echoed in her head, so much clearer this time.

"Yes, it's time I left this behind." Olivia felt a euphoric feeling come to her and everything dissipated. She closed her eyes and when she opened them again, she found herself in the white void once more.

"Well?" Haniel asked.

"It's worse than I remember it to be." She sighed and Haniel sat down next to her.

"We can talk about that."

"What is there to talk about?"

"First of all, it's best not to dwell on the past."

"I know, but I just can't forget," Olivia said.

"I'm not asking you to forget the past. I'm just telling you to move on from it. Keep him alive in your memory, but don't let his death hurt you like it did before."

"Well, that's easy for you to say," she whispered. "You're an angel. All you know is goodness and happiness. Have you ever lived a day like us? Like a regular person on earth?"

"No, but I've lived for centuries while being able to see devastation everywhere I went." Rather than feeling offended, he stayed indifferent. "I've been sent to help you and Brennan. I don't want you to think I'll just leave you two out in the cold."

Olivia gently pushed him away and turned her back towards him. "Why? Why am I still alive? Why couldn't you just let me rot in hell like every other suicide victim?"

"I guess God has a plan for you."

"That's the most clichéd thing you could've said," she laughed. "There's obviously no reason for me to be here. What would you do if I killed myself again?"

"You don't have to. Trust me on this. If you give up after all you've been through, you'll regret it for the rest of forever." Haniel's eyebrows drooped and he put a frown on his face.

"There's a lot more for you to learn, and once you reach the end of that line, you won't regret it. Living through this will give you a certain drive you've never felt before."

Olivia clenched and unclenched her fists. Coming to terms with her past and living in the present was something she truly wanted. "Is that true?" she asked.

"Yes, yes, it is. Once you wake up from this coma we'll get back into things and it'll all pick up again. Just take some time to rest now." Olivia felt Haniel put his arm around her, but she used her shoulders to push him away. "Olivia, you have to understand that —"

"I know," she interrupted. "I need to move on, but I still don't know how to do that. Everything has been going downhill. My mom and I don't even talk to each other anymore." Olivia felt the weight of her hands on her weak knees. She lay on her side and stared off into the distance, and even though her hands trembled, Haniel was there to steady them. She became still as her eyes looked dead, and pretty soon sleep invaded her like a parasite.

Chapter Eleven

When Brennan opened his eyes, he felt a soft fabric surrounding his torso. He looked down and found himself wearing a completely different outfit. Rather than the shirt Jessica had let him borrow, he wore a white blouse with a light blue mini skirt. A few of the top buttons on his shirt were undone, and Brennan noticed a significantly large bruise on the side of his neck. He used his arms to push himself up, but felt a stabbing sensation in his pelvic region. Not only that, but a sensation made his body feel like dirt.

It was as if only a shower made from the tears of an angel could wash away the filth, but nothing more could be done. As he heard the clattering of dishes from the kitchen, he rolled off the couch. With a heavy breath, he managed to push himself to his feet. His eyes scanned the shabby old house, and his mind drifted with intrusive thoughts. *Why did he feel pain around his pelvis? Why were the top buttons on his shirt undone? Why was there such a large bruise on his neck, and most importantly, what was this disgusting, violating feeling running across his body?* For a moment Brennan had to put a hand over his mouth before he screamed out in terror, and luckily for him, he managed not to scream. His head turned to the stairs, and he briskly ran up the steps with light feet. Normally at his mother's house, his feet would echo though the halls, but this time they were completely silent, almost as though he were a cat.

Once he got to the top of the stairs, he found himself standing in front of three doors along a crooked hallway. On the right side were two doors and on the far left stood another. Brennan lightly touched the knob of the first door and opened it. Inside the room was a double bed, and a dresser with pictures lying on top of it. Out of curiosity, he moved forward to get a good look at them. All the photos were polaroid shots of Olivia passed out. In some, she looked like a regular person fast asleep, while in others, she resembled Sleeping Beauty. In those pictures, she was indistinguishable from a comatose patient. The way her body looked like a corpse and the fact that she was put in odd positions made it obvious that she wasn't put to sleep naturally.

While Brennan stood scanning each photo, he heard the clatter of dishes slowing down, so he decided to leave the room just as he left it. He silently shut the door behind him before walking further down the corridor. He opened the second-last door, only to see a bathroom, but something in the trash caught his attention. He stepped inside and locked the door behind him.

Inside the garbage bin was a pile of rubber condoms, some empty and others used. Immediately Brennan took off his blouse and stared at himself in the mirror. He hadn't noticed it before, but now he could see the bruises and red marks on his lower abdomen. Upon further inspection, he realized that the marks were imprints of large hands that must've tightly gripped him. Tears started to well up in his eyes and he gritted his teeth. He slapped his palms on the counter and twitched his fingers. After everything he'd been through, this is what it had come to. He looked at his wet face in the mirror, but the sight of his reflection made him want to punch it – to shatter the glass so that he wouldn't have to see himself like that anymore.

He ran over to the toilet and lifted the seat. He stared into the bowl, wishing that he could drown himself. Eventually, his chest started to rise and his throat gagged, but no bile came out. He wanted to throw up, but he couldn't. He shoved two fingers down his throat until he started gagging. He continued to apply pressure until he puked water. With nothing else being able to be forced out, he laid his back against the wall and sobbed. Everything just seemed to make sense now. The perverted stepfather, the bullies at school, and the absent mother. Olivia's life must've been hell, and the severity of it became more than what Brennan could handle.

Stop crying. Stop crying, he told himself. He wiped his red eyes and slapped his temple. "Get up. Soldier on," he chanted.

From there, Brennan stood up from the position he was in and walked out of the bathroom. He opened the door across the restroom and ended up entering a whole new world.

In contrast to the rest of the house, the room had no odor, and the walls were a dark shade of pink. A computer was placed on a desk against the wall with a bookshelf standing next to it. Alongside the novels on the top shelf were journals that filled the bottom portion of the rack. Brennan picked up the most recently dated one and skimmed through the pages. Most were mundane passages, but some provided more context to Mr. Benning.

I hate him. I just hate my stepdad. Can you imagine having someone torn away from you, only for them to be replaced by some monster trying to take their place? Every morning when I wake up, I always feel like gravity has a stronger pull on me. It's like my head is being pulled down by strings. I know he has something to do with this, but I can't seem to prove it. My mom says teenagers always sleep. They sleep all day, every day, but this can't be normal. One time I even woke up in a new set of pajamas. I went off my stepdad after that, but it's my word against his, and my word is worth nothing. I can't stand this town. Island Bay. Just the name of it is traumatizing. This town might as well be a prison. You could smother me with a pillow, and it'd be similar to how this town feels.

Brennan shut the journal after reading the entry.

I need to get out of this house. He paced back and forth while thinking of an escape plan, but all that was cut short when he heard a knock on his door.

"Olivia, are you in there?" Mr. Benning asked. For a moment, Brennan didn't respond. He hoped that ignoring him would make him go away, but Mr. Benning just knocked harder and louder. "Open the door. We need to talk."

"Uh, hold on." Brennan threw all the books and journals on the floor to lighten the rack. He went over to one side and began pushing it towards the door.

"What's all that racket!?" Mr. Benning yelled.

"I'm just changing my clothes. I'm looking through my closet."

"Bullshit! What are you doing in there?" Mr. Benning began to wiggle the knob before throwing himself against the door. His body slammed against it repeatedly, and with each strike, the wood began to crack.

"Hold on, I'm still changing!"

"It doesn't take that long to change. Just be honest with me and open up."

"I can't, my bra is stuck," Brennan lied. By now his arms felt weaker than noodles, but the shelf was almost against the door. He just needed a bit of a push. Rather than saying anything, Mr. Benning slammed himself against the door, and Brennan saw a crack appear.

"Fuck off!" Brennan yelled. By now, he finally got the shelf against the door. He ran towards the window and unlocked it. When he opened the glass, cold air brushed against his skin, but the cold felt like freedom. He popped one leg through before turning around to see a hole being punched through the door. Mr. Benning put his face against it and started screaming at Brennan to come back. Brennan gave him the middle finger before jumping out of the window, but the jump didn't come without its consequences. When he hit the ground, the force made him topple over. By now, Brennan was covered in scrapes and bruises, the most notable one being on his right elbow. Blood dripped from the wound, but he still picked up the pace and ran down the street.

For a considerable amount of time, Brennan marched on the sidewalk, past various houses. None of them showed any signs of life. Their curtains were closed, blocking anyone from viewing the inside. Eventually, darkness covered the sky, with blotches of white surrounding the moon. Brennan wondered what time it was and how long he had been running. Hours? Minutes? Who knows? Maybe by now, people were lying down in their beds, or maybe the night had just begun.

Brennan let his guard down, believing that Mr. Benning wouldn't find himself anytime soon, but he knew that if Mr. Benning didn't kill him, the cold surely would. Going out in a blouse and skirt exposed him to the elements, and Brennan found himself shivering.

He took the first house to the right as a place for salvation. He strode up the four steps to the front door, leaving behind his footprints in the grass. He raised a finger to the doorbell and pressed it. The dinging sound of an electric bell could be heard ringing throughout the house, but the lights never turned on. He rang it again, but nothing changed. The house remained dark, with no signs of life. Not even the driveway had a single vehicle in it, and while he stood there, the coldness began to seep through his shirt. His body slowly became numb as the sensation passed through the rest of his body. Considering that he was being pushed to the brink of hypothermia, a locked door wasn't enough to stop him. He scoured the premises for a spare key. First, he checked under the doormat, but nothing came of it. He gave a sigh as he waddled around the front yard. Apart from the lawn being a massive expanse of overgrown grass, gravel seemed to lie below the windows. His feet crunched over pebbles, with each step grating on his ears.

He stopped and turned to face the house. The lower half of the walls was made of bricks, while the upper half was built with wood. He knelt down to examine the workings of the bricks. His hands ran across them until he felt one jutting out of the wall. Upon inspecting it further, he found it to be removable. He slowly pulled it out, revealing a key that was hidden inside. He immediately snatched it and opened the front door. He pushed himself through and fell to his knees. For once during the past hour, he felt warmth. It was the same kind of warmth a child would feel in their mother's arms. Despite the cold granite flooring, the rest of the home harbored a milky white carpet.

With trembling legs, Brennan gradually stood up. He closed the door behind him and proceeded to collapse on the couch a few feet in front of him. Even though he feared the reaction of the returning homeowners, he still let the exhaustion consume him. Mentally, Brennan willed himself to get up and search for a landline, but what he did physically was another story. Rather than listening to his mind, he snuggled his face into a pillow and fell asleep.

The night went by silently until Life chose to make an appearance. Since Brennan forgot to lock the entrance, she found an easy passageway into the home. As he lay there on the couch, Life hopped on his stomach. As soon as the tip of her toes made even the slightest weight, his eyes popped open. He stared down his chest and aimed his eyes at her.

"What are you doing?" he asked in a groggy voice, but Life just continued to stare at him. "Well, are you going to tell me why you're here? You always seem to hang around me at the most inconvenient times."

"Mr. Benning is looking for you."

"Yeah, I figured that would happen."

For a moment they both paused and stared at each other. For whatever reason, her rounded face and wide eyes still pierced through him in the darkness.

"You should leave," Life pestered, but Brennan just gave a sigh.

"Sure, but let me sleep first." He rubbed his eyes, trying to fall asleep, but Life slapped his chest.

"Hey!" Brennan yelled.

"God didn't give you a second chance just so you could just waste it." Life sounded more adult-like, which caught Brennan's attention.

"Oh, I forgot about him. By the way, what's he been doing this entire time? Is he just sitting up there high above as my life falls apart?"

"He's waiting for the right moment," Life said.

"Well then, he's an asshole. I've been busting myself trying to fix things, and all you can say is, 'He's waiting for the right moment,'" Brennan mocked. "I can tell you – he's never been there for me. Where was he when I lived with my mom? Where was he when Mr. Benning hovered around Olivia? I can tell you, action is stronger than faith."

"Don't say that," Life whined.

"Say what? That he abandoned me? There's nothing he can do for me now. If he really cared, he'd make sure Olivia and I were in our own bodies again, but look at us now."

"Just wait and see," Life pleaded.

"Like I said, action is stronger than faith. I'm not going to wait around." Brennan waved her off and closed his eyes, hoping to get some sleep, but she wouldn't get off him.

"Wake up." She leaned forward and placed her tiny palms on his chest to shake him. "Wake up, Brennan."

"Stop. Let me sleep so I can feel dead again."

"But Olivia and your sister need help."

Once he heard the word "sister", Brennan quickly opened his eyes. "My sister is the one who left me. You're telling me she needs my help now? Of all the times she could've returned, now is the time?" Brennan looked down his chest and saw Life nodding her head.

"Olivia's in the hospital again, and Nora is –"

"Just forget about it. I can't help anyone while I'm stuck like this."

Life frowned and made a pouty face. For a moment, neither one of them said anything. It was just Life's strong glare and Brennan's avoidant gaze.

"Let me at least get a few hours of sleep. Please. I just want to forget what happened today. We'll deal with this later."

Chapter Twelve

Just before the rise of dawn, a bright beam of headlights pulled into the driveway. The glare traveled to the sofa and shone onto Life's face. Its strength caused enough of a stir to wake Brennan, but Life slapped his chest to just to make sure.

"Someone's here!" she whispered in his ear. Rather than jolting his body up, he casually rolled his head to the side with a glazed look in his eyes. Despite the impending threat, Brennan's consciousness still wasn't up to the task. He tried to roll over to put himself to rest, but Life raised her hand to slap him. Just as he was about to scream at her, she placed a hand over his mouth. Even though she only covered two thirds of his lips, it was enough to get her message across. "Someone's coming!" she whispered again.

Finally, Brennan hustled off to the back of the couch to hide his body while Life ran in a completely different direction.

As the door swung open, the cold immediately became apparent. The returning homeowner plopped himself down on the couch. With Brennan staying hunched under the side of it, he waited for the right moment to escape. Once the man's eyes finally shut, Brennan jumped at the opportunity to leave the residence. He quietly walked his way out the door with light footsteps before breaking into a complete sprint. In front of him was a road that stretched endlessly in both directions.

"Brennan!" Life called out. She stood in the park across the street, waving her hand up high. The small beam of sunlight looming over the horizon acted as a guiding path. Without looking both ways down the street, Brennan slowed down his pace to a light jog as he crossed the road.

Once he got to the other side, Life took hold of his hand and led him towards a play set. "Let's play," she said.

"I don't have time for this," Brennan said. "Let's go."

"Where are you going?" she asked.

Brennan stopped for a moment to ponder. He came to the conclusion that she was right. Where was he going? Definitely not back to Olivia's house. Not with Mr. Benning lurking there. "Life," Brennan said as he knelt down, "where's Olivia?"

"She's back where she started."

"What's that supposed to mean?"

"Olivia doesn't seem to be sleeping again." Life let the words roll off her tongue as she put a finger to her lip.

"Wait a minute," Brennan said fearfully. "Don't tell me she's dead."

"No, just in another place. She's been like that since yesterday."

"But where is she? Is she still in Florida?"

Life shrugged her shoulders.

"Oh my god, if you're some all-seeing child, why can't you just give me a solid answer?" Brennan gripped her tightly by the shoulders before vigorously shaking her.

"Stop!" she whined.

"Just tell me what you know!" Brennan yelled.

As he continued to agitate her, a tear came flooding down her face. "Stop, you're hurting me!" Rather than slapping his chest, she aimed for his face and made contact with it.

He flinched before saying, "Hurt..." That word was all he could think of. "I'm sorry, I just..." The words began to roll out of his mouth. "Sometimes I just..." While he took a knee, Life did nothing but wipe her eyes.

"You're just like –"

But before she could finish her sentence, Brennan interrupted her. "I know. You don't have to say it. I'm sorry. I've always promised myself that I'd never turn out like my mom, but I failed."

"That's not true," Life said.

"Are you sure about that?"

She nodded. "But you're still mean."

Brennan heaved a heavy sigh and got back on his feet.

"Let's just forget about this for now. Do you still want to play?" Despite his attempts to raise her mood, she just shook her head while keeping her eyes aimed at the floor. "Fine, let's go." He extended his hand out to her which she grabbed. Brennan led the way, all while he felt a heavy weight gripping his ankles. Each step became harder as the guilt began to grow on him. *Not like her. Not like her,* he repeated to himself.

"Brennan, why do people like you exist?" Life asked.

"You know, I had a similar conversation with Jessica, and I'm still trying to figure that out. Maybe we're just molded into the person we are. Maybe that's why we exist... But then again... Why do the people who made us this way, exist?" Suddenly Brennan felt even guiltier than he had already been. To say that he was molded this way made him feel like he was placing blame on someone else, and after spending time with Jessica, he realized he needed to take responsibility for his actions. If she could do it, then so could he.

"People like you are —"

"They're just like my mom, huh?" he muttered. "I don't know. Do you think people like me are the bad guys?"

"I think so," Life said.

"Well, now that I think about it... Maybe we're not the 'bad guys'. Maybe we're just sad. Not 'bad', but 'sad'. Maybe we just have a bad coping mechanism."

"But why are you so sad?"

"If I had to guess, it would be my mother. I guess isolation just isn't my thing."

"Was your mom also sad?"

"I never thought of that, but now that you mention it, maybe she is. Although I wonder why she'd be sad."

Despite the usual lack of answers, Life finally decided to provide one. "What if you were the one to make her sad?" she said.

"But how? What did I do to her, and was that enough to justify what she did to me?"

"Well, do you think your sadness justifies your actions?"

For a moment Brennan stopped to look down at her. "I guess not. People don't really need much of a reason to do anything. Let's just see where we end up from here." Due to his lack of rest, he knelt down to the grass and begged Life to stop with him. He fell sideways and curled into the fetal position. With Life sitting next to him, he stared up at the sun peeking over the clouds.

"Life," Brennan said, "since I've been given a second chance, does that mean God loves me?"

"Do you believe in him?" she asked.

"After everything I've been through, yes. Of course I do, but I'm starting to think he doesn't believe in me. I know I believe in him. There's no doubt he's real, but does it matter if he hates me? After all, isn't it obvious that relationships can't be one-sided? Maybe he doesn't despise me, yet in that case I'd still reject him for all the shit he put me through. Or how about this? Maybe I love him for giving me a second chance, but he wouldn't love me. He'd still hate me for becoming the person I am." Brennan moved his eyeballs towards Life to gauge her reaction, but she didn't show anything. "I had an aunt who went to church every Sunday," Brennan continued. "Each time I spat out words of hatred towards my mom, my aunt would scold me. All I ever heard from her was 'Repent, repent, repent'. That's all I heard, and for a while it was the most putrid word in my vocabulary. 'Repent'." Brennan spat on the ground. "But sometimes I think, she's right. I'm not sure, but I think she sees me as some sort of monster. A monster that should kneel before God and beg for forgiveness. It's like she wants me to apologize to my mom, when in reality, she should be apologizing for turning me into a monster." Brennan rolled over on his back and took one last look at the sky. "God, I need to get to Olivia."

After the sun became clearly visible, Brennan woke up from his short nap. By then, Life had disappeared like she always did, and once again, he was alone. The thought of Mr. Benning clouded his mind. The search was on. He knew that by now that man must've dropped everything to search for his daughter. Definitely not for sentimental purposes, but instead to fuel his own perverted fantasies. Brennan considered the fact that Olivia lived in a small town, therefore he thought it'd be best to flee the area as soon as possible. But where would he go? He looked across the street to see the homeowner of the residence he'd broken into. The man had gone outside to water his front lawn. The seemingly mundane act of watering dead grass became more exciting when Brennan noticed the bicycle parked next to the gate. Without hesitation, he marched across the road with ill intentions.

"Good morning," the man said, completely oblivious. But rather than saying "Hi", Brennan hopped on the bike and pedaled down the pavement in a straight line. The man shouted after him. However, Brennan was quick to create enough distance for the man's voice to quickly become inaudible.

Now what? The idea of pedaling forever seemed impossible, but then again, everything that happened so far was the exact definition of insanity, but all the wrongs he'd done and all the wrongs he'd experienced, gave his legs the fuel to keep going.

Despite the exhaustion, he managed to pedal until he came across the community library. It sat atop the massive hill he'd conquered. For the time being he hopped off the bike and let it hit the ground.

As he stepped through the front doors, he immediately arrived at the front desk. "Do you have any books about this town?" he asked the elderly librarian.

"Silly girl. I remember you spending ages looking through our old archives. Just last month you told me about a story you're writing of a town resembling ours." The librarian laughed, but all Brennan could give was an uncomfortable smile.

"Well, can you remind me where the archives are? After all, it's been a while since my last visit." Brennan eyed her shirt until his eyes rested upon her nametag: *Brenda*. "Please, Brenda. I could really use your help." Brennan made sure to sweeten his tone.

"Oh, alright. In the back of the library near the Non-fiction section, you'll find a shelf near the study area. The books go from 200 to 300, according to the Dewey decimal system."

Even though Brennan had no clue what that was, he gave a big smile and headed towards the end of the library. He kept an eye out for text with photos and famous people who were recorded in history. Pretty soon he completely forgot all about the numbers and went by pictures like he normally would. Eventually, he arrived at a section with maps and noticed that each one shared the town's name. *Island Bay,* they all read. His eyes looked through all the dates neatly labeled on the map until they rested upon the most recent one. He pulled it out, revealing that the way out was a bridge that connected the island to the rest of Washington. He traced his finger from the building all the way to the bridge. He took a moment to rotate it around to make sure no one was keeping tabs on him. Once it became clear that he was completely invisible, he shoved the map into his blouse.

When he marched out of the library, he pulled out the piece of paper to take another peek at it. No doubt the bike wouldn't be enough, but what else could he do? He began to mentally list his options of people who could help him. *Mrs. Benning, Mr. Jefferson.* However, he brushed all of them off in favor of Jessica. When he remembered that she had a car, he gave out a sigh of both relief and stress. She was probably the only person who'd be willing to help him, but he still needed to give her a reason to. He folded up the map and put it back inside his blouse.

Right then, a patrol car caught Brennan's attention. The officer rolled down his window.

Is he looking for me? Not wanting to find out, he hopped on the bike and cycled as fast as he could out of the parking lot. Figuring that Jessica would probably be at school, he pedaled faster towards the academy.

As he rode towards the school, the sun began to rise ever so slowly in the sky, until it reached its peak at noon.

Once Brennan entered the school's parking lot, he jumped off the bike, and with his pulse pounding, he searched for Jessica's vehicle. The longer he stayed there, the more students would stare at him.

"Olivia!" Brennan heard a male voice shout.

Oh shit. In a panic, Brennan turned his head toward the voice, only to see Mr. Jefferson waving his hand while running toward him. Brennan also noticed a familiar woman walking around, and yelled Jessica's name, hoping that it was her. The girl quickly turned around and sure enough, it was her.

She ran to him in a light jog. "Olivia, what are you doing here? I heard that you –"

"Forget about that," Brennan interrupted her. "Just get me the hell out of –"

Before he could finish his sentence, Mr. Jefferson placed a hand on his shoulder. "What's going on here?" he said. "The police questioned me. According to your father, you ran away."

Instead of responding to him, Brennan walked toward Jessica and placed his arm around her shoulders. "Take me away, please," he begged.

"Now hold on a minute!" Mr. Jefferson said. He raised his hand to signal for silence. "I can't let you go. I'm required to report your appearance here. After all, children don't just run away for no reason. Something's on your mind again."

After his lengthy tirade, Brennan didn't offer any words, but he did crane his neck to look at Jessica. "If you want to right your wrongs, you'll take me out of here," he told her.

Upon hearing that, Mr. Jefferson scolded Jessica. "I see then," he said. "I guess Jessica has something to do with it. Come on, I'll take you to the counselor." He beckoned for Brennan to follow, and tightly gripped his arm to drag him away.

"Jessica, please," Brennan screamed. "I can't stay. They'll take me back to my dad! I know we've had some problems but please, listen to me! I need you."

After his cries, Jessica stepped in. She placed herself between the two of them. She used both her arms to push them away from each other, resulting in Brennan falling over. She offered her hand to help him up, which he graciously accepted. "Mr. Jefferson," she said. "Obviously something else is happening in her life. Don't you want to consider what she's saying?"

"That's why I'm bringing her to the counselor, and I can tell you: running away with her won't solve anything."

"Jessica, don't listen to him," said Brennan. "I know what I'm saying sounds crazy, but you have to trust me. You've already gotten an impression of who my dad is. Didn't you meet him in the emergency room, and don't you remember everything I said about him?"

By then, all eyes were on her. Mr. Jefferson had a bemused look while Brennan held puppy dog eyes. He stared at Jessica, begging her to take him away, but she finally lost her decisiveness. "Jessica, please," he begged. "I need to get out of here. You have to help me!" Despite not being one to beg, this time was different. Rather than being the tough guy he always portrayed, the inner child within him was beginning to take over. "Please. Please help me, please."

"Just hear her out," Jessica told Mr. Jefferson. "I have met his father, and I genuinely believe he's abusing her."

"You believe, or you *know*?" Mr. Jefferson retorted.

For a moment Jessica turned her head away.

"I understand that you kids are having it rough but remember we can always talk things through." He gave a fake smile, but Brennan knew it was just a front.

"I can't wait! I have to go now!" Brennan yelled. "I'm sorry," he whispered to Mr. Jefferson.

"What was that?" Mr. Jefferson asked. Then, without saying a word, Brennan struck him in the groin with his knee, and threw a punch at his face.

"Olivia, what the fuck are you doing?" Jessica yelled. "He might've been right. Maybe we could've just talked and gone to the police!"

"No time to argue," Brennan said. "Just trust me on this. We need to leave now. Get in your car and drive me to Florida. We're getting the fuck out of here."

"I can't –"

"Now!" Brennan yelled.

Jessica sprinted to her car, with Brennan running around to jump into the passenger's seat. Once they locked all the doors, Jessica shoved the key into the ignition.

"Hit the gas, now!"

And with that, Jessica swerved out of the parking lot onto the road.

"Look, Olivia... I trust you, but you have to tell me what's going on."

"It's complicated," Brennan said. "Even if I told you, you'd never believe me."

"Why?"

"Because my journey so far has just been one big fever dream."

Jessica eyed him. Ever since Brennan had taken over Olivia's body, he'd brought chaos to everyone around him, especially Jessica. Even though his fear of leaving her held him back, it didn't anymore. He knew that to keep her around in this endless cycle of chaos just for his sake was selfish. *I have to get to Olivia...* Although he didn't know how to fix the mess he already made for her.

Chapter Thirteen

The longer the drive went on, the more Brennan yearned for peace. With him yelling obscenities at Jessica and Jessica yelling back, he became mentally exhausted. Even though he knew this was his fault, he just wanted a miracle to stop it.

"Let's take a moment to calm down," Jessica said.

For a moment Brennan caught himself. Sure, he had a good enough reason to panic, but since his childhood years were over, he hadn't really felt the need to do that. Most of his anxiety came out as anger rather than a full-blown panic attack. Yet here he was, on the verge of hyperventilating. "You're right. I'll just stop talking for now." Brennan rubbed his forehead with his thumb and index finger while he laid back in his chair. He breathed out a sigh and folded his arms across his chest. He felt an awkward pause between them.

"So, why don't you tell me your side of the story?" Jessica said. "Maybe that'll give me an idea of what to do next."

"Like I said, you wouldn't believe me even if you saw it happen," Brennan sighed.

"No matter what, I promise I'll listen," she told him.

Brennan recounted all the events from his perspective that had led up to the present moment. From his suicide, and waking up at the train station, to the fact that he and Olivia switched bodies, everything finally came out. Jessica might not have believed him, but one thing was certain. Brennan felt amazing to be able to vent to someone.

"That sounds impossible and insane," Jessica said.

"Like I said, you wouldn't believe me." Brennan rolled over on his side and looked out the window, thinking about what to do next. If Jessica didn't believe him, what would she do? Would she turn him in to the police? Surely his dream of driving all the way to Florida would be dead by then. "I know you're probably doubting me, but at the very least, don't leave me alone. I can't go back to my house. I can't go back to school, and I definitely can't go back to my stepdad." Eventually, this became one of the few instances where Brennan showed vulnerability.

"Listen, you sounded genuine when you told me what you told me, but I just can't believe it. But I don't want to abandon you. Even if you are insane, I won't leave you."

Brennan's eyes grew wide after hearing her words, and he looked at her with a newfound kind of love. "Thank you. Thank you," he cried.

Even though Jessica's decision had elated him, he still wondered what her intentions were. But for now, he decided not to question or complain about it. All that mattered was getting the help he needed.

Olivia was stuck in limbo. By now, she was living in her own world where anything she could think of could come to life. She imagined the white void turning into her father's house. Everything from the floor to the specks of dust on the kitchen counter became an exact replica. The front door had an assortment of colors, while a brown doormat lay in front of it. Shoes were strewn across the wooden floor, and the kitchen was littered with cabinets on the wall. Ever since her escapade into her mind, she spent a considerable amount of time at the dining table. She imagined her father and herself eating with a generous plate of food. Right now, she picked at her plate with a fork and rested her chin in her palm.

"Having fun?" Haniel asked as he snuck up behind her.

Olivia turned around and greeted him with a smile. "I wish I could stay here forever," she said.

"Unfortunately, you can't. Once this coma is over, it'll be time to get back on your feet." He gave a big grin while Olivia rolled her eyes.

"I know, but... Why can't I just stay here?"

"I know this is what you want, but this isn't what you need," Haniel said.

"You're right. I just wish I could relive my childhood again. I just wish things were different."

Haniel took a seat at the dining table. "What are your plans? When you get out of here, I mean?"

"I think I'll just work on getting better, physically. Then I'll meet up with Brennan. Maybe then this will all be over... But I've been thinking about something..."

"Oh, and what is that?" Haniel asked.

Olivia stood up and began pacing the room to help her think. "Once this ends, what will happen to us? Will we ever see you again? Will Brennan and I stay in contact?"

Haniel took a deep breath. "We can worry about that later."

"But we can't," Olivia told him. "I can't just sit around waiting for an answer. I need to meet Brennan once I get better."

"But how can you?" Haniel asked her. "How can you, when you don't have a plan?"

"I'll find a way." For now, Olivia sat in her chair, wondering what to do. Her world had turned upside down, and yet here she was, just waiting. The curiosity about how Brennan lived his life invaded her. She tried to conjure an answer for how he could be so assertive and decisive.

"Hey, Haniel."

"What is it?"

"Do you know what my biggest fear is?"

"No."

Olivia swallowed and said, "I'm scared of forgetting how I initially felt about each person I meet. I remember when I met Brennan, I thought he was just some hot-headed guy, but that doesn't seem to be the case anymore. Now, I'm starting to consider everything Brennan said. I'm starting to doubt myself again. Maybe I am weak. Maybe Brennan's right. I have to grow a backbone to be more assertive. Meanwhile, I'm stuck here wondering why Jessica is tagging along with him."

"What are you trying to get at?"

"I just hate feeling clueless. I hate feeling like I have no control. When I think I know someone well, it's like I have some sort of control. It's like I can predict what will happen next, and they won't pull a trump card on me. I thought I knew myself and my life. I thought nothing would ever change... that everything would stay as it always was. But now, everything's different, and I don't want it to be different."

"You can't dwell on the past."

"I know I can't, but I can wish, can't I?"

Haniel looked away instead of answering her.

"Sometimes I think that if I can wish hard enough, anything can come true, but that's not true, is it? I thought the world could love me like it used to, but it's changed too." Olivia gritted her teeth and clenched her fist. The burning desire to act on her own began to etch itself on her face. "I can't wait any longer. Once this coma ends, I'll be out of here. I'll do whatever it takes to find him."

"Olivia," Haniel said, "you don't sound like yourself."

"I know I don't, but being here and having all this time to reflect is driving me insane. Brennan's right. I need to take more action."

Haniel smiled at her and together they waited until she woke up.

After some more of Brennan's crying and guilt tripping, Jessica finally came to a decision. "Olivia," she said, "we'll go to my house first to pick up a few things for our drive. I think it'd be best to –"

"Just make it quick," Brennan pleaded.

"Don't worry. I will."

Jessica drove through the small town, taking the fastest route back to her parents' house, but to Brennan, something seemed off. After every turn they took, the sound of police sirens could be heard in the distance. The sound of them, along with their screeching tires, burned themselves into Brennan's ear, and despite the morning sun glaring down at them, their emergency lights shone brighter. The entire town was dotted endlessly with patrol cars at every corner, and the idea of going back to Jessica's house didn't feel right to him.

"I think we should just go," Brennan said. "We need to leave as soon as possible."

"I think you're right."

Once they reached the roundabout, Jessica made a U-turn onto a clear road. She pushed harder on the gas pedal until the speed meter reached 70 miles per hour. Her hands wrapped themselves tightly around the wheel until her knuckles turned white.

"Jessica," Brennan said. "Don't grip the wheel like that. You'll end up going off the road."

"I'm sorry," she said. "I'm just a little scared."

"In that case we're the same."

For the next twenty minutes, the ride went on uneventfully, with Jessica keeping her eyes on the road while Brennan's attention veered off to the window.

However, by the time they arrived at the bridge, everything changed. Apart from the usual fog and forest, there were a couple of patrol cars parked on the side of the road.

"Olivia," Jessica said.

Brennan turned his head to look at her, and suddenly understood what she meant. He nodded and rolled his body down the chair.

"Yeah, just stay hidden for now," she told him. She continued to drive forward, with her face staring straight ahead. They were able to get the car on the bridge without garnering any attention. As the wheels drove over the concrete, Brennan took a moment to sneak a peek out the window. It seems that the town was really built on an island. Under the bridge and miles beyond, stretched an ocean with a few islands spreading themselves out over the distance. Brennan sat there wondering if Olivia ever left her hometown, and if so, did she admire the view just as much as he did? For once in his life, his heart fluttered at something that wasn't a beautiful girl.

"Wow!" he whispered to himself.

Jessica looked at him and gave a short chuckle. "You had that same look when we left for that field trip to Seattle."

"I guess so," Brennan said. He brushed off the knowledge that Olivia had left the town before. He was just too enamored of how beautiful the scenery was, but once they left the bridge, a small amount of sadness tugged at his heart. He lay back in his chair and closed his eyes. Jessica hummed a familiar tune he heard on the radio, before he drifted into a vivid dream.

"What is this place?" Brennan asked himself. "Where am I?" Even though his body stayed asleep, his mind had taken him elsewhere. He found himself lying at the edge of a lake next to a waterfall. His back arched, along with the shape of the rock, and the sun beat down brightly on him.

Jessica lay on her stomach by his side. It seemed they had both stripped down to their underwear. Their garments were soaked and drops of water still swept across their forehead.

Brennan sat up to look all around the misty forest. The sight and warmth radiating from the sun made him curious. How could it be so foggy yet so sunny at the same time? Rather than making that idea one of life's greatest mysteries, he lay down again and poked Jessica on the cheek.

She opened her eyes and a grin spread from ear to ear. "I was taking a nap," she said.

"I'm sorry."

"No, it's fine. Was there something you needed?"

Brennan looked up to the sky and pondered his thoughts. "Can't think of anything right now. Something about you just seemed important to me."

Jessica chuckled and rolled onto her back. She stretched her arms out and yawned, before lying still like a board. "I didn't turn in that poem to Mr. Jefferson."

"What poem?" Brennan asked.

"The one I asked you to help me finish when you spent the night at my house. Don't you remember?" Jessica sat up and towered over him. For a moment they stared into each other's eyes before she broke it off with another smile. She crawled towards their clothes strewn out on the grass at the edge of the lake. Her hand hovered over her pants until she shoved it in her pocket. She pulled out a piece of paper with writing scrawled all over it. She walked next to Brennan and sat down. "Can you read it for me?" she asked.

Brennan turned his head and carefully took the note from her hand. His eyes squinted to read it, but all the words seemed to float around the page. "Uh... Life is –" Brennan struggled to read. "Life is inevitable," he read. The title felt like a bowling ball striking his heart. He felt something deep inside him stirring up. The sensation originated from his stomach, so he tried to push down, but nothing happened. Eventually, his body shot straight up. He coughed before dropping the paper into the water and puking out a stream of clear liquid. In the stream of vomit lived fish, tadpoles, and an assortment of foliage. Even though he was puking entire ecosystems, Jessica just stared at him.

"Sometimes I feel like water is clogging up my lungs," she said. "It's like I want to speak, but I can't. I know what words to use, what expressions to show, but... Nothing will come out. It's strange, isn't it? Is this what it's like to bottle everything up? Is this what you felt when you took your life?" Jessica looked at him once more, but Brennan was too busy vomiting to utter a sentence. "The water burns and my lungs scream. Everything I say, and everything I want to say is just algae being swallowed by fish, and then those fish get eaten by bigger fish, and then it's nothing. Just complete silence, and that silence is just so deafening. Isn't it strange how silence can be deafening? After all, silence is just silence, but not to people like us. To us silence can be an assortment of things. From words to screams, to feelings, to friends, silence is everything. I'm sure you know how that feels. Don't you?"

Brennan's stomach stopped pushing out that disgusting stream of water. He coughed up nothing but pain for the next minute.

"Jessica, what are you–?"

Before he could finish, the sun shone brighter and the mist began to roll in. The sunlight on heavy fog resembled an oil lamp. The air became gray and warm at the same time.

"Brennan..." Suddenly Jessica's tone of voice became heavier. "... save me." A small trickle of blood started to ooze from her forehead, just below her hairline. She stood up, only to fall to her knees. The blood started to pour out like a river. At first, it went down the left side of her face, and once her face became drenched in blood, the rivers of red began to wind in a snake pattern down her face. Like a leaf stem, they went everywhere. She crawled towards him with her entire body shaking.

"Jessica..."

She fell into his arms and together they went down to the bottom of the lake.

Brennan woke up alone in the car. His eyes gazed upon the area, and he realized that the sky took on a dark color pallet. Their vehicle was parked next to the gas station, and with Jessica missing, Washington's hard winds became even more ominous. The only light source he had was the streetlamp hanging above the car.

"Jessica," Brennan called out. After receiving no response, he called out to her again.

"Look!" she happily screamed, running out of the gas station. Brennan glanced at her arms to find nothing but snacks and energy drinks. "We've got a long drive ahead of us," she told him. "You should eat something. Here." she tossed him a box of chocolates. Brennan fumbled with it in his hands until it rested easily in his palms. He laid back and opened the box while Jessica filled the gas tank. From chocolate bars with nuts to milk chocolate, everything he wanted was there. He smiled to himself and took a look at Jessica. Within a couple of minutes, their tank was completely full.

She immediately jumped in the driver's seat and they sped off down the road.

"How long have we been driving?" Brennan asked.

"Well, since we left at about early morning, I'd say it's probably been eight hours."

"I think we should find a motel to rest for the night."

Chapter Fourteen

After the hour had ended, an old inn finally came into view. To find it, they had to take a detour from the busy highway. The road curved down a hillside and into a foggy expanse of trees. The decrepit building appeared to have been built ages ago.

Jessica took the first step out of the vehicle with Brennan following closely behind. As they strode together, he shivered, while Jessica stayed composed. Not a single part of her body shook, except for her hands. When Brennan looked down at them, he noticed sweat appearing across her palms. *Why was she sweating?* With the breeze being this cool, there was no reason for heat to pass through her hands.

"Are you feeling alright?" he asked her.

"I... I am," she hesitated.

"Are you sure? I know this trip was very sudden, but you can always vent out to me. I've already asked for a lot. I just want to make sure we're on the same page."

They continued talking as they inched closer to the entrance, but Jessica paused once they reached the door.

"Do you think it's too late for me to turn things around?" she asked.

"What do you mean?"

"I mean, is it too late to turn my life around? Is it too late to turn myself into a different person? Because to tell you the truth, I don't like who I am."

"Why are you being so sentimental all of a sudden?"

"It's just that... ever since I started spending more time with you, I've been trying to be more self-reflective. I don't know. It just seems like everything is different. You're different. I'm different. And my whole world is different." Jessica's face drooped over to one side and her lips turned upside down.

"I think we should get some rest first." Brennan placed a hand on her shoulder and together they entered the inn.

The inside was filled with specks of dust floating above the lamps that illuminated the place.

A certain smell immediately became present and lingered in the air. Brennan couldn't identify it, but he surmised that it must've been common to all elderly buildings.

Sitting at the front desk was a young girl who had fallen asleep in her armchair.

Brennan walked forward and gently tapped his finger against the wooden surface. The girl woke up and looked at him in bewilderment. "Oh, I'm sorry," she said.

"That's okay," Brennan told her.

"Hold on, I'll be right back." The girl ran around the desk and up the staircase, calling for her mother. She kept screaming "Mom!" until a woman who seemed to be in her late thirties came down. The woman peered around the corner and Brennan caught her gaze.

"Hi there," she said.

"Hi, we'd like to rent a room for the night," Jessica told her.

The woman nodded and made a circle to the desk. She asked for their names and for payment.

Embarrassed by his lack of resources, Brennan blushed when he realized his pockets were empty.

Jessica stepped in and paid the amount that was owed.

Unfortunately for them, they discovered that the room they rented only had one bed, but that didn't deter them. After all, sharing a mattress was something they'd already done, and the power of sleep deprivation had a stronger force than social norms.

Jessica went over to the left side of the bed and sank in while Brennan collapsed on the right side. Once he laid down, he took the time to feel the foam and velvety sheets.

"Olivia?" Jessica said as she rolled over to face him.

"What is it?"

"I just want you to know that I'm sorry. I'm sorry for treating you the way I did."

"Don't worry about that now. Everything is fine. You've already done more than enough to help me. You've done more for me than anyone else has."

She smiled at Brennan's response before averting her gaze. "You say that, but I still remember all the times you told me about your dad. You know... your *real* dad."

Brennan thought for a moment and wondered what Olivia's father must've been like. He knew that he was a strong presence in her life, but suddenly that knowledge put him on edge. It felt like a fire he wanted to snuff out.

"Why don't you tell me what I told you. It would make me happier to hear those stories again," Brennan said.

"Well, you always said your dad was a writer. You told me that he could write about anything. That each letter naturally turned into a word and each word created its own unique world. Apparently, every world became massive, with characters of all sorts. Some of them changed over time, while others didn't at all. You always talked so much about him. You talked about him like he was still here, and I can't say it didn't make me jealous."

"Jealous? What do you mean?"

"Just forget about it." Jessica turned over again so that her back was facing him.

"No, I want to hear more," said Brennan, tapping her shoulder. "Tell me what's on your mind."

"I guess all I can say is that there have been more bad memories than happy ones when it comes to my dad, but at least I remember the happier ones more clearly. You know, one time, in particular, my dad was telling me a bedtime story to put me to sleep. I must've been five at the time, and it's embarrassing to say, but back then, I always thought there were monsters lurking under my bed or hiding in the corner, but my dad was always there to comfort me. He told me a story about a king who loved his daughter so much that he would slay every monster standing in their way. By the end of the tale, he told me, 'Monsters aren't real, but people who act like monsters are real. I just want you to remember that even monsters are capable of acting like people and people are capable of acting like monsters.' After that, I asked him why, but he just told me, 'Some people see a monster and do whatever it takes to destroy it. In fact, you'll probably feel that way at some point in your life, but don't become so blinded by your own hatred that you turn out worse than the monster you seek to destroy.' I didn't know what he meant at the time, but now I'm starting to think I do." After Jessica told her short story, her voice trailed off.

"What does it mean?" Brennan asked.

"Are you asking about the story my dad told?"

"Yes." Brennan could feel Jessica shift her body weight as she dug her face deeper into her pillow.

"I'll just say that if he were still here, It'd be a story about us."

Before he could probe her for more answers, he felt her body go limp, and when he looked over her shoulder, she was fast asleep. As she slept, Brennan felt the strong urge to wake her and reveal his true identity – to come out as Brennan Claufield rather than hiding behind the façade that was Olivia Benning, but that dream would probably never come true, and so Brennan brushed it off before turning in for the night.

Just like in the car ride, Brennan awoke within a vivid dream. This time he saw himself standing in front of a mirror. The water from the sink poured endlessly, and Brennan's face was soaked, but when he looked into the mirror, he noticed a line running down the middle of his face. The left side of his reflection would be Olivia, while on the right was an image of his real identity. That side of him had black hair, while the other side had red hair. He put his hand up to the glass and looked down at the sink. Suddenly the water stopped running, and a strong, disgusting taste filled his mouth. His stomach began pumping something upwards until he puked it all out. Murky water flowed out of his mouth and down the drain. He could taste pieces of dirt and rocks on his tongue. Numerous fish swam around in the stream. Some were munching on the dirt, while others chased each other around in an endless cycle.

Despite being a short experience, it still felt like ages until it ended. But after that, he looked up to see the mirror turn into a window. It appeared to be located at the bottom of the lake, and showed a view upwards out of the water. Fish floated about and a giant waterfall was shooting down on the glass. Eventually, bright rays of the sun shone into his eyes. Brennan tried to put his hands over his face, but nothing could stop the beam.

However, as it made the liquid more transparent, Brennan noticed a note floating around in the water. It made its way up against the glass. *Life is Inevitable* was scrawled on top, but the rest of the page became a black mess of running ink, and as that blackness filled the lake, it did the same to his vision.

Brennan woke to the sight of the sun beaming through the window. Everything seemed to be in order, except for the fact that Jessica was missing. Brennan got up and looked all around the room. Eventually, he went down the stairs to be greeted by the young girl again.

"Hello," he said.

She looked up from her comic book. "Do you need anything?"

"I'm looking for my friend. You know, the girl I spent the night with?"

"I saw her go outside. Said she just wanted to go for a walk."

"Thank you." Brennan stepped out the door, but the girl called him back.

"Just be careful," she said. "One time we had a guest go down the waterfall, off the side of the hill."

"I'll keep that in mind." Brennan strode out the door and into the misty forest. He wandered aimlessly while calling out to Jessica. A few moments after the leaves crunched beneath him, he heard Jessica scream along with the splashing of water. Fearing the worst, he sprinted towards the sound, but came to an abrupt stop when he saw Jessica swimming in the lake. As it turns out, she didn't fall at all. In fact, it seemed more like she just walked down the side of the hill and stepped into the water.

"You scared me!" Brennan yelled at her from the top of the hill.

"Come down here and join me!"

With that, Brennan marched down the trail until he came to the base of the waterfall. He stripped down into his underwear and hopped in. He swam out to Jessica until they were face to face. By now, she was all smiles while Brennan's body shivered.

"Aren't you cold?" he asked her.

"Nope, not at all."

"Well, I still don't want to be here for long. After all, we've got a whole country to cross."

Jessica turned her head away and looked down with despair in her eyes.

Brennan reached out his hand and lifted her chin. "Is there something wrong?" he asked.

"No, nothing. Let's do something else. How about playing Marco Polo?"

Before Brennan could question her further, she began the game. They played for a few rounds, and each round they listened to each other's screams. One would yell "Marco!" while the other would yell "Polo!", and by the end of it, Brennan was exhausted by laughter.

"This is a great change from yesterday," he said. "It's nice to take a break after running from everybody. You seem even better than me. What changed?"

"I guess I just needed some time to rest. I felt too tired to do anything. At least now I've got some energy back." From there, Jessica swam to land and pulled herself out of the water.

Brennan promptly followed her and together they lay on their backs facing the sky. Even though the ground was made up of one large solid rock, neither one of them minded.

"I haven't had this much fun in a long time," Brennan admitted. "God, I wish more days were like this."

"There'll definitely be more days like this. I promise you that." After her words left her, she heaved a big sigh.

"There's still something wrong, isn't there?"

"What makes you think that?"

"It's just a gut feeling, but you tend to sigh when something's wrong."

She chuckled at his comment and rolled over to look at him. "You always seem so empathetic to others. I'll definitely miss you."

"What do you mean 'miss me'? We're traveling together."

"I mean I'll... I'll miss you once the trip is over," she stammered out.

For a moment, Brennan felt grief. He knew that he'd have to leave her behind. "Yeah, I will too, but once we get to Florida, I can introduce you to my friend, and then we'll be one big team. Like the Three Musketeers." Despite having to actively think when talking about himself in the third person, he'd gotten so used to acting as Olivia, that it had become an easy feat.

Jessica gave him a weak smile and thanked him. "What's your friend like?" she asked.

Brennan imagined the way his sister might've described him to her friends, and so he assumed that persona when talking about himself. "Well, his name is Brennan, and you two are actually very similar. He might seem a little scary, but I get a feeling he's changed and matured quite a bit. We're all a bit different, I guess."

As he spoke, a tear slowly started to form in the corner of Jessica's eye. Brennan watched it slowly roll down her face.

"There's something bothering you, isn't there? You can tell me." Brennan reached out his hand and wiped her face.

Initially, Jessica denied the accusation, but after some more pressure, she gave in.

"I just don't know what I'll do when this is over. I know you want me to run away with you and Brennan, but right now our situation is more complicated than that. I mean, everyone probably thinks I just kidnapped you. Either that or... I just assisted in harboring a runaway. I don't think I have anywhere to go. I just left home, and my family probably doesn't think too highly of me anymore. I don't know what to do, Olivia." The way she ended her sentence made Brennan's heart melt. He could feel her sense of control wavering, and her eyes reminded him of the same eyes he had as a child. Just a frightened kid who had no one else to turn to.

"Don't worry. I'll stay with you, always. How about we dry ourselves off and get back to the inn?"

"I'd rather just wait here for a while," she said.

For a moment Brennan hesitated, but after noticing her distress, he decided to just stay by her side. He lay on his back and pretty soon, as he became accustomed to the temperature, the cool air became warm air, and he made sure to take in every bit of the atmosphere. Eventually, the gradual onset of warmth persisted until he fell asleep.

By the time Brennan woke up, the sun had reached its peak height for the day. Despite the new feeling of eternal warmth, a strange feeling washed over him. Something in the back of his mind told him that now wasn't the time to sleep. When he looked to his side, Jessica was nowhere to be found. Even though her disappearing had become a common act recently, this time felt different. Her presence still lingered long after she vanished.

Brennan got up and began to put his clothes back on. As he did so, he wondered what the future could hold for him. What would happen once he and Olivia returned to their bodies? Would he return to his old life, assuming that all the chaos would eventually end? After all, even though Brennan hated to admit it, he had created a hectic life for Olivia to follow up. Considering the massive fight he had with her stepfather, and the fact that he became a runaway, he doubted she could return to anything resembling normalcy, and once he put his clothes on, he fell flat on his bottom, just to stare into the water.

He took in Olivia's face, wishing it were his own. He kept pondering what to do until he decided enough was enough. He stood tall and began to walk to the side of the hill, but a piece of paper floating in the wind caught his eye. It went up and down while doing a few curls before he snatched it out of the air. At first, it was blank, but once he turned it over, he realized that a whole poem seemed to be written on it. He read the title. *Life is Inevitable.* And pretty soon, he recognized the familiar handwriting. The smoothness and femininity of it all could only point to one person: Jessica.

"Jessica!" he called out, but no answer came. The longer the silence ensued, the more his brain would conjure the deepest, darkest scenarios he could think of. "Jessica, come here!" Still, silence filled the air, only to be broken by Brennan's voice once again. "Jessica, where are you?" He turned his head in different directions, but he couldn't even catch a glimpse of her face.

"Marco!" Even though Brennan anticipated her to yell "Polo!" right back at him, her voice was still nonexistent. "I said, *'Marco'!*"

Still no answer.

Brennan's heart raced, with his blood pumping to the beat of the waterfall. He put the note down and ran into the lake with his clothes on. "Marco! Marco! Marco!" With each silent response, his fear grew wider and wider. He swam to the waterfall hoping to find her, but nothing resembling life came into view, just a bunch of rocks being devoured by the water. "Jessica, please," he muttered to himself.

He sniffled, and a tear rolled down his eye, camouflaging itself with the droplets of water. He swam towards the rock that he and Jessica had slept on, and gazed all around the valley.

"Marco!"

Brennan stared out into the distance, hoping to find her, but the only thing that remained in his vision was the scenery, until he heard something hit a rock a few meters away. He turned his head to see a pale-white girl lying lifeless against the stone. He swam out to her and pulled her close. "Jessica...?" He shook her, but she didn't even flinch.

He pulled her out of the water and laid her on the grass. A tiny sliver of blood ran down her forehead, all the way to her chin. In a panic, Brennan slapped her face, hoping she'd wake up, but she didn't. Fearing the worst, his mind went back to various dramatic scenes he'd witnessed in the movies he'd seen growing up. He imitated one of the characters performing basic resuscitation, but to no avail. Her body was still cold, and blue.

For now, he knew, Jessica was dead.

He felt a mixture of anger, hatred, and guilt. And all those emotions were directed towards himself. He felt angry at himself for committing suicide. If he hadn't done that, nothing would've acted as a catalyst for this event. He also hated himself for bringing her into this. *I shouldn't have gotten close to her.*

But most importantly, he felt guilty for being himself. By now he'd realized just how pathetic he really was. He wasn't a tough guy. He was just an angry little boy running around, thinking he was hot shit.

He knelt by her side and held her hand in his. He gave her a short kiss on the cheek and stood up. He knew his journey wasn't over, and that he needed to move on, but the thought of leaving her just seemed too barbaric. He wrung out his hands so that they were dry and placed Jessica's palms over her chest. With her more serene appearance, he picked up the poem she'd written and read it on his way back to the inn.

Life is Inevitable
The air around me still feels like a cage
This cage holds torment
This cage holds innocence

This cage holds chaos
Torment is nothing more than the restraints that led me here
Innocence is the life that once was
Chaos was the rioting of mental violence I've suffered
But there was a key
That key came in the form of a battered bird
She opened the cage and forgave me
She tore off a wing of her own and handed it to me
She freed me
For life is inevitable
Just as inevitable as death

After reading the poem, Brennan carefully folded it and held it is his hands. By then, he was already halfway to the door of the inn. The sun still shone high as though nothing awful had just taken place. But eventually, the wind started to howl, and the environment became more fitting.

Brennan burst through the door with bloodshot eyes. Instead of coming face to face with the little girl, he was met by the sight of her mother, seated at the front desk staring at him.

"You look horrible," she said in disbelief.

"Call for an ambulance. My friend… my girlfriend… just died in the lake."

The woman immediately ran to the phone hanging on the wall and dialed 911.

After that Brennan stormed up the stairs to grab the car keys, before heading outside again. Once he stepped out, he ran towards Jessica's vehicle and put the key into the ignition. He drove off into the distance.

By the time he felt overwhelmed, he stopped by the roadside. Enough was enough. No more death, and no more crying. Even though the ocean of tears wasn't dry anymore, Brennan felt the need to build a dam to block it out. The time to reach Olivia was now, and Brennan couldn't wait any longer. He gritted his teeth and came up with a plan to execute.

Alright, he told himself. *Let's go.*

He pressed hard on the gas pedal and sped forward. The speed meter did nothing but rise each second, and as each second passed, Brennan bit harder on his lip. His canine tooth dug itself deeper into his flesh until the tip of it stabbed through. He could taste his own blood, but by now he had the heart of a lion. He screamed as the vehicle reached its top speed, but eventually, fog began to envelop the road.

The streetlights hanging above slowly dimmed out until they were completely nothing.

His headlights disappeared and he was left in the mist.

Brennan slowly stepped on the brake pedal. The sound of his tires skidding across the pavement echoed, as though he were in a valley.

When the car came to a complete halt, he got out and looked into the distance.

The fog rolled in without hesitation, and with it, came a warm feeling of nostalgia, but rather than trembling at the sight, Brennan closed his eyes and took a deep breath. He let the mist surround him. It slowly stretched over his body like a blanket. At first, it only covered his feet, but it gradually traveled up until his body wasn't visible anymore. He felt slender arms wrap themselves around his chest, and a feminine voice whispering in his ear, "I am light and easy, but the longer I live with you, the heavier I become. What am I?"

"What is that supposed to mean, and who are you?" Brennan asked, but received no response.

Instead, the arms hugging his chest became lighter until he couldn't feel them anymore.

The fog felt warmer and warmer. The sound of dozens of voices and trains bombarded his ears. Once he opened his eyes, the mist became filled with a warm glow. It started off as a faint light illuminating a small area in the distance, but as time went on, that orange glow slowly crept towards him, and the fog began to disappear.

The endless mist wasn't so misty anymore.

Black cobbled walls began to show themselves along with train tracks, and the ground beneath him revealed itself to be carved out of cobble as well. Ticket booths made of wood started to appear as the fog vanished, and that's when Brennan noticed all of the people walking around.

There were dozens of men, women, and children everywhere. Some were sitting on benches, others were milling about, some were waiting in line for a ticket, and the rest were boarding trains.

"Well, here I am... back at this stupid train station."

Brennan walked over to a bench and sat down on the middle of it. He stretched his arms out wide and leaned back. The dam he'd built to block out his tears broke, and pretty soon the surface of his eyes became an ocean. He was blinded by his own tears. He couldn't see anything, but that was when he heard footsteps coming his way.

"I can see you for who you really are," a feminine voice said.

"Jessica? Is that you?"

Thank you for reading *Life is Inevitable*! Next year we'll see the end of Brennan's and Olivia's journey through the afterlife and self-discovery. Go to my website and sign up for my newsletter to receive notifications and updates for the creation of *Hated by Life*, the next novel in the series.

https://www.dantheauthor.com